MEDITERRANEAN DOCTORS

**Let these exotic doctors
sweep you off your feet...**

**Be tantalised by their smouldering
good-looks, romanced by their fiery
passion, and warmed by the emotional
power of these strong and caring men...**

MEDITERRANEAN DOCTORS
Passionate about life, love and medicine.

Dear Reader

My husband and I love to travel, so when I came up with the idea of writing two books about twin sisters it seemed the perfect opportunity to use two of our very favourite places as settings for the stories. Bill and I spent our honeymoon in Sardinia, so that had to be one of the places I chose, and then last year we went to Cyprus for our wedding anniversary and had a wonderful time there, so I chose that as the second location. We've had great fun looking through all the photographs together.

Katie and Kelly Carlyon have a lot in common apart from being twins. They both work in the world of medicine and they have both fallen in love with men who live in the Mediterranean. Whilst Katie flies to Cyprus to be with the man she loves, Kelly moves to Sardinia to forget about the man who has broken her heart. However, as they soon discover, life doesn't always work out the way you hope it will!

I really enjoyed writing the two books in this mini-series, and hope that you will enjoy them too. You can read Katie's story in DR CONSTANTINE'S BRIDE. Kelly's story will be published later this year, so do look out for it.

Love

Jennifer

www.jennifer-taylor.com

DR CONSTANTINE'S
BRIDE

BY
JENNIFER TAYLOR

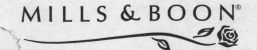

First published in Great Britain 2007
Harlequin Mills & Boon Limited,
Eton House, 18-24 Paradise Road, Richmond, Surrey TW9 1SR

© Jennifer Taylor 2007

ISBN-13: 978 0 263 85238 7
ISBN-10:   0 263 85238 5

Set in Times Roman 10½ on 12¾ pt
03-0507-51829

Printed and bound in Spain
by Litografia Rosés, S.A., Barcelona

Jennifer Taylor lives in the north-west of England with her husband Bill. She had been writing Mills & Boon® romances for some years, but when she discovered Medical Romances™, she was so captivated by these heart-warming stories that she set out to write them herself! When she's not writing, or doing research for her latest book, Jennifer's hobbies include reading, travel, walking her dog and retail therapy (shopping!). Jennifer claims all that bending and stretching to reach the shelves is the best exercise possible. She's always delighted to hear from readers, so do visit her at www.jennifer-taylor.com

Recent titles by the same author:

THE WOMAN HE'S BEEN WAITING FOR
A NIGHT TO REMEMBER
A BABY OF HIS OWN*
THE CONSULTANT'S ADOPTED SON*
IN HIS LOVING CARE*

*Bachelor Dads

PROLOGUE

'I AM *REALLY* going to miss you!'

Katie Carlyon hugged her twin sister Kelly. Now that the time had come for them to part, she was feeling extremely emotional. They had never been separated for any length of time before and it was going to take some getting used to.

'I'm going to miss you too, but it's all in a good cause.' Kelly hugged her back, her green eyes sparkling with laughter. 'Admit it, Katie, you're dying to see Petros again, aren't you?'

'Yes, I am.'

Katie laughed, hoping her sister couldn't tell how uneasy she felt. She still hadn't heard from Petros. He hadn't phoned her or replied to the numerous text messages she'd sent him in the past few days. They hadn't spoken, in fact, since she'd told him what time her flight was due to land. She understood how busy he must be in work, but surely he could have found the time for a brief phone call?

'Ah, love's young dream.' Kelly chuckled. 'It makes you feel all warm and tingly inside.'

'Just you wait, Kelly Carlyon,' Katie threatened. She certainly didn't intend to worry her sister when they were both on the verge of starting a new life. Petros had told her that he loved her many times and there was no reason to doubt him. 'I'll get my own back when you fall head over heels in love!'

'You'll have a long wait because it's never going to happen. I've had my fill of romance, thank you very much.'

Katie was about to protest but at that moment her flight was called. She hugged her sister again then picked up her bag. 'I'll text you as soon as I get there. Take care.'

Katie hurried to the security desk and showed her boarding pass then made her way to the departure gate. It was the beginning of May and there were a lot of people going away on holiday. Cyprus was a popular destination and the flight was full; she had to wait until her row was called before she could board the plane.

Twenty minutes later the plane took off and she watched as England disappeared under a veil of clouds. In four hours' time she would begin a new life with the man she loved. It was a big step, but she was sure it was what she wanted to do. She wanted to be with Petros for ever more.

CHAPTER ONE

WHERE was he?

Katie could feel her heart thumping as she keyed in the phone number of the hospital. There'd been no sign of Petros at the airport when her plane had landed. She had been waiting for over an hour now and he still hadn't turned up. She had tried his mobile phone several times but it was switched off. The only thing she could think of was to phone him at work.

'Poseidonos International Hospital. *Kalimera.*'

'I wish to speak to Dr Constantine, please,' Katie explained as calmly as she could. She waited while her call was put through, praying that Petros would be there. Although he had told her about the villa he owned in the coastal town of Paphos, she had no real idea of its location and wouldn't attempt to make her own way there. If she couldn't get in contact with him then she didn't know what she was going to do…

'Dr Constantine.'

The man's voice cut through her mounting panic and she heaved a sigh of relief. 'Petros, it's me—Katie. Oh, I am so glad to hear your voice!'

'I'm sorry, but there has been a mistake. My name is Christos Constantine.'

'Oh, excuse me,' Katie said hastily. 'I didn't realise there were two doctors by the name of Constantine on the staff. It's Petros I want to speak to. Would you be kind enough to have my call transferred? My name is Carlyon—Katie Carlyon.'

'And why do you wish to speak to him, Miss Carlyon?'

'I think that's my business, don't you?' Katie bridled at the arrogant note in the man's voice. Now that some of her initial panic had subsided, she could hear the difference. This man's voice was much deeper than Petros's voice. It also didn't hold that hint of amusement which she always found so attractive.

'No, I don't. It is very much my business, in fact. Petros warned me that you might show up. However, if you imagine that I am going to let you ruin his wedding day, young lady, you can think again.'

'Wedding day,' Katie repeated numbly. 'I don't understand. Are you saying that Petros…that he's getting married?'

'Of course. Don't pretend that you didn't know. Petros assured me that he had told you about Eleni in the hope that it would put an end to all this nonsense. He has been distraught about the number of messages and phone calls you have made to him recently.'

'I have no idea what you're talking about! I've never even heard of Eleni. Petros certainly never mentioned her to me. The last thing he said to me was that he loved me.'

Katie bit her lip when she felt tears well in her eyes. She had no idea why this man was saying such things. Petros loved her—he did! But if that was the case, why was he planning on marrying someone else?

She took a deep breath, fighting down the feeling of dread that filled her. 'I need to speak to Petros so we can sort this out. Please have my call transferred to his office.'

'I have no intention of allowing you to hound my cousin, Miss Carlyon.'

'Hound Petros? If anything, it was the other way round. It was Petros who bombarded *me* with invitations to go out with him!'

It appeared that her claim must have held the ring of truth because there was a brief pause before the man said curtly, 'Where exactly are you calling from?'

'The airport. My flight landed just over an hour ago and I've been waiting here for Petros ever since.' Her voice caught when it struck her it was unlikely that Petros was on his way to meet her if what this man had said was true. Just for a moment the enormity of what was happening engulfed her. She had given up her job and her home to start a new life with the man she loved but it appeared that he no longer wanted her. It took a huge amount of effort to focus as the man continued speaking.

'Stay there. I'll come and find you. It will take me about twenty minutes to get there, maybe a little longer if I get held up in traffic.'

'How will I recognise you?' she said quickly, but he'd already hung up.

Katie took a deep breath as the line went dead. It was all very well for him to tell her to wait until he arrived, but she couldn't stand here and do nothing. Maybe she should telephone the hospital again, only make sure that she asked for *Petros* Constantine this time. It had to be some sort of mistake, of course. She really couldn't believe that Petros had said those awful things about her. She only had to remember the number of times he had told her that he'd loved her to prove that.

After all, it wasn't as though she had rushed into an affair with him. She had always been extremely cautious when it came to relationships. Watching their parents go through an acrimonious divorce while she and Kelly had been growing up had left its mark, and Katie knew it was the reason why she had been so wary about getting involved in the past. Although she had been out with several men, she had always refused to be rushed into a relationship. She hadn't wanted to find herself in the same position as her parents had been in.

Her mother and father had met and married within a few months. They hadn't taken the time to get to know one another and cracks had soon appeared in their marriage when they'd discovered that they'd had very little in common. When their daughters had arrived the following year it had put an added strain on the relationship. Katie had been ten when they had divorced and she had prayed that it would put an end to all the arguments, but it hadn't happened.

There had been more fights, over custody this time. Then, once it had been decided that she and Kelly should live with their mother, there had been rows every time their father had wanted to see them. Life hadn't settled down until she and Kelly had been old enough to leave home, and by that time the damage had been done.

Katie had made up her mind that she would wait until she was sure before she committed herself. She knew that she had gained a reputation in the hospital where she'd worked as a staff nurse for being very choosy when it came to men, but it hadn't worried her. She didn't intend to take any chances.

When she'd first met Petros, she hadn't been overly impressed. He'd been working on the exchange programme and he'd seemed rather too keen on enjoying himself to take him seriously. When he had asked her out, she had refused, but he had asked her again and had kept on asking her until in the end she had agreed.

She had always been rather quiet, but Petros had drawn her out of herself and made her laugh. He had been so handsome and so charming, so different to the other men she had known that she had found herself falling in love with him. Even then she had held back, but when he'd told her that he had loved her, too, she had been completely won over.

When Kelly had announced that she was taking up a new job in Sardinia, Katie had realised it was time that she made some changes to her life, too. Petros had just returned to Cyprus and she was missing him dreadfully. The thought of being left behind in England without him or her sister had been more than she could bear so she had decided that she would go to Cyprus to be with him. After all, he loved her and she loved him, so what was the point of them being apart when they could build a future together?

That had been her plan right up until the time her plane had landed. It was *still* what she wanted, in fact, so was she really going to give up her dream of finding happiness on the strength of what some stranger had told her?

She started to key in the phone number of the hospital again then hesitated. Maybe she had believed Petros when he'd told her that he'd loved her, but what if it hadn't been true? What if it had been merely a ploy to get her into his bed? It wouldn't be the first time a woman had been taken in by claims of undying devotion so how could she be sure that it hadn't happened to her?

All of a sudden doubts started crowding into her head and she was no longer certain of anything any more. She cancelled the call and put her phone in her bag. It might be better if she waited to hear what Dr Christos Constantine had to say before she did anything.

Christos swore softly as he hurried out of his office. This was the last thing he needed! It was difficult enough to pretend that he was genuinely delighted that his cousin was marrying Eleni without having to deal with this kind of complication as well. Just for a second he wondered if he should phone Petros and tell him to sort out his own mess, but then he thought about Eleni, and how much it would upset her if she found out about this woman, and realised he couldn't do it. He cared too much about Eleni to risk her getting hurt.

'I have to go out for a while so I'll need you to take charge of the department, Yanni.'

Christos stopped by the desk to speak to his senior registrar, Yanni Papadopoulous. The emergency department had been unusually quiet that day and he had been intending to use the time for some in-house training. The team had been together for only six months and it was important that their skills were constantly assessed. There were a couple of new nurses who had started that week and he was particularly keen to put them through their paces, although there was no sign of them, he realised.

'Where are the new nurses?' he demanded.

'Tina had to go home because her little boy was sick, and Rachel didn't turn up this morning,' Yanni explained. 'We phoned her apartment and someone there told us that she'd gone back to England.'

Christos sighed. It wasn't the first time they'd had problems with staff from abroad. The idea of working in another country might be appealing, but the reality often proved to be vastly different. Although the weather in Cyprus was a huge improvement on that in the UK, it didn't make much difference when you were working gruelling twelve-hour shifts.

'I'll get onto the agency when I come back and see if they can find a replacement. I shouldn't be long—an hour at the most. If anything urgent crops up, page me.'

He left the hospital and got into his car. It was just gone noon and the roads were fairly quiet for once. Although Cyprus attracted large numbers of tourists all the year round, the real rush wouldn't start for another couple of weeks. That was when his department would really come under pressure.

As head of trauma care at Poseidonos International Hospital, Christos had seen at first hand the effects too much sunshine and wine could have on people and there was very little that surprised him nowadays. He dealt with every case with the same degree of professionalism. He had worked hard to reach his present position, adhering strictly to the path he had laid out for himself after his parents had died. They had both been doctors, too, and it had seemed only right that he should honour their memory by following them into the profession.

It had been a long and arduous journey because he had been determined to reach the very top, but he could confidently say that he had achieved everything he had set out to do—in his professional life, at least. It was his private life which was such a mess, and there was little he could do about that.

The thought sent a pang coursing through him as he drew up in front of the airport, but he couldn't afford to worry about his problems right now. He had no idea what he was going to do about Katie Carlyon, but he wouldn't allow her to ruin Eleni's wedding day. Even though at one point he had hoped that Eleni would marry him, he had accepted a long time ago that it would never happen. Eleni deserved a husband who would be there for her, someone who would put her needs before everything else.

He had been far too focussed on his career since his parents had died. Even when they had been teenagers, and Eleni had used to beg him to go swimming with her, more often than not he had refused. It had been Petros who had accompanied her to the beach; he'd been too engrossed in his studies.

The situation had continued throughout his time at university. It hadn't been until he had been in his first job that he had admitted to himself how he felt about her. Maybe he could have dealt with his feelings if Eleni hadn't made it clear that she was attracted to him, too.

They had started going out together and it had been wonderful at first, but gradually it had become apparent that the relationship wasn't working. He'd been working excruciatingly long hours at the hospital and they'd hardly seen one another. Whole weeks would pass when he had been too busy even to phone her. When Eleni had told him that she'd decided they should split up it had been unbearably painful, but he had known in his heart it was the right thing to do. Eleni had deserved more than he could give her.

It had been ten years now since they had gone their separate ways and time had helped to heal the pain. However, it had still come as a shock when he had found out that Eleni was dating his cousin. And it had been an even bigger one when she and Petros had announced their engagement shortly after his cousin had returned from working on the exchange programme.

Was Petros really the right man for her? Christos wondered

not for the first time. His cousin had always enjoyed playing the field and it was hard to believe that he would remain faithful to her for the rest of his life. Christos had had serious misgivings from the beginning but he had kept them to himself for Eleni's sake. After all, Petros claimed that he was madly in love with her so who was he to disagree? Although after what Katie Carlyon had told him earlier, he had his doubts. If Miss Carlyon had been telling the truth, then his cousin's idea of love was vastly different to his own!

Christos sighed as he got out of the car. There was no point worrying about it right now. Maybe he did have his doubts but he would do everything in his power to ensure this wedding went ahead as planned. And if that meant sending Katie Carlyon back to England, that's what he was going to do.

Katie scanned the faces of the people coming into the terminal, although she had no idea how she was going to recognise Dr Constantine when he arrived. Would he look like Petros? she wondered. He'd said that Petros was his cousin so there might be a family resemblance.

Her eyes skimmed over a tall, dark-haired man who had just entered the building and she felt a frisson run through her. Although he didn't really look like Petros, there was something familiar about those chiselled features. She followed his progress as he made his way across the concourse. In contrast to the tourists in their colourful holiday clothes, he was soberly dressed in a lightweight grey suit with a white shirt and a discreet blue tie. He looked big and commanding as he stopped and stared around, and Katie suddenly felt afraid.

Did she really want to suffer the embarrassment of having him harangue her again? Maybe he'd felt those comments he'd made had been justified, but he hadn't even asked to hear her side of the story. He had no idea what had really gone on, how Petros had pursued her with single-minded determination. He had judged her and obviously found her lacking so what was the point of giving him the chance to do it again? It would be far more sensible if she avoided another confrontation and went to the hospital and asked Petros what was going on.

Katie snatched up her case and headed for the door at the far end of the terminal. She knew from watching the other visitors that she should be able to get a taxi there to take her to the hospital. In her heart, she still didn't believe that Petros had said all those horrible things about her. For all she knew, that man could have made them up for reasons of his own, and the thought added wings to her feet. She needed to see Petros and find out the truth!

She had almost reached the exit when a woman suddenly screamed. Glancing round, Katie could see an elderly man lying on the ground, clutching his chest. She hesitated, torn between a desire to see Petros and the need to help, but in the end her conscience wouldn't allow her to walk away. Hurrying over to the couple, she put down her case and knelt beside the old man.

'What happened?' she asked, her hands moving automatically as she loosened the collar of his shirt.

'I don't know.' Tears were streaming down the elderly woman's face. 'Frank said that he had a pain in his chest and the next thing I knew, he collapsed.'

Katie nodded as she pressed her fingers against the carotid artery in the old man's neck. She sighed when she failed to detect a pulse. His heart had stopped and if he was to have any chance at all then she needed to start CPR immediately.

'I'm a nurse,' she explained, rolling him over onto his

back. 'Your husband's heart has stopped so I'm going to give him CPR. Can you phone for an ambulance and tell the paramedics that it's a cardiac arrest?'

The woman went to pieces when she heard that and started sobbing. Fortunately, someone in the crowd had heard Katie's request and offered to make the call. Katie left them to get on with it; she was more concerned about maintaining the patient until help arrived. Permanent brain damage occurred when the brain was starved of oxygen for longer than four minutes.

She checked the man's airway was clear then tipped back his head and gave four sharp inflations then checked his pulse once more, but there was still no sign of his heart beating.

'I'll do the compressions. You continue with the breathing.'

All of a sudden the man whom she'd seen entering the terminal a few moments earlier was kneeling beside her. He didn't look at her as he deftly performed five chest compressions then paused. Katie breathed into the old man's mouth again, forcing herself to concentrate on what she was doing. She couldn't afford to be distracted when a man's life depended on her actions.

They carried on for what seemed like ages—she breathed into the man's mouth while the stranger performed the chest compressions. An eerie silence had fallen over the terminal as more people gathered around them to watch what was happening. Everyone was willing them to save his life and Katie knew that it wouldn't be for lack of effort if they didn't succeed.

'Pulse check.'

The stranger rapped out the instruction and Katie immediately obeyed as her training kicked in. Placing her fingers on the carotid artery, she felt for a pulse and smiled when she detected the faintest movement beneath her fingertips.

'We've got a pulse,' she said, unable to hide her delight.
'Good.'

Something crossed the stranger's face, a flicker of some
emotion that looked almost like surprise, before he returned
his attention to their patient. Once they were sure the old man
was stable, they rolled him onto his side and placed him in
the recovery position. They had just finished when the ambulance crew arrived.

Katie quickly told the paramedics her name and explained
what had happened then moved out of the way. They fitted
the old man with an oxygen mask then set up a drip and lifted
him onto a trolley. The crowd was starting to disperse now that
the excitement was over so she picked up her case and edged
away. With a bit of luck, she might be able to disappear...

'I'll take that.'

A large hand suddenly lifted the suitcase out of her grasp.
Katie didn't have time to object as the stranger put his other
hand under her elbow and hurried her after the trolley. The
ambulance was parked right outside the main doors and he
paused only long enough to give the crew some instructions
before he led her to his car.

'I'm sorry but I'm not going anywhere with you,' she said
firmly, wrenching her arm out of his grasp. She took a step
back and pointed to her case. 'Please, give me my suitcase.'

'Later, after we've had a chat.' He stowed her case in the
boot then opened the passenger door. 'I am Petros's cousin,
Christos Constantine. We spoke earlier on the phone. I don't
have time to deal with you at the moment so please get into the
car.'

'No.' Katie shook her head. 'I just told you that I'm not
going anywhere with you. You might claim to be Petros's

cousin but why should I believe you? You could be anyone for all I know.'

He slid his hand inside his jacket and pulled out his wallet. 'Here is my hospital security pass. As you can see, my name is Christos Constantine and I am the head of trauma care at Poseidonos International Hospital. Unfortunately, I don't have any more identification on me at the moment, but I shall be happy to provide you with further proof once we reach the hospital.'

'You're taking me to the hospital!' she exclaimed.

'Yes.' He opened the door wider. 'The choice is yours, Miss Carlyon. However, I don't have time to stand here arguing with you. There is a man on his way to hospital who needs my help, so please make up your mind what you intend to do.'

CHAPTER TWO

CHRISTOS was glad that Katie Carlyon didn't seem inclined to talk as they drove to the hospital. He wasn't sure if he would have been able to carry on a conversation with her. He had gone to the airport, sure in his own mind about what he would find. After all, he'd seen any number of Petros's girl-friends over the years and they'd been of the same ilk—pretty, empty-headed women whose only interest in life was their own comfort.

His gaze skimmed sideways and he frowned as he took stock of the delicate purity of Katie Carlyon's profile. There was an innate sweetness about her expression which surprised him. He'd also been impressed by the way she had gone to that man's aid so promptly. She definitely didn't fit the usual mould of one of Petros's girlfriends, although he couldn't allow that fact to influence him. Although he had long since recognised that his cousin wasn't a saint, he had believed Petros's claim that Miss Carlyon had been making his life hell. It seemed that actions as well as looks could be deceiving and it was a salutary lesson when he remembered the way he had responded to her. There'd appeared to have been such delight in her eyes when they had managed to stabilise the old man, but he mustn't make the mistake of thinking it had been genuine. Katie Carlyon may look like an angel, but the image was only skin deep.

'Which department is Petros working in now?'

The question caught him unawares. Christos answered it without pausing to consider the wisdom of what he was doing. 'He has returned to the surgical unit.'

'Oh, good! That's what he was hoping to do.'

Katie Carlyon's voice was filled with warmth and he frowned when he felt a tremor run through him again. He had no idea why he should respond to her this way, but he didn't appreciate being made to feel so vulnerable. His own tone was deliberately brusque when he replied.

'Petros was extremely lucky to be given a second chance. Not many heads of department would have taken him back after what happened.'

'What do you mean?' Katie stared at him in surprise, and Christos laughed.

'Ah, I see my cousin didn't tell you that he'd been suspended. Perhaps you two weren't as close as you thought you were?'

He saw her flush but she returned his gaze and he had to give her credit for that. 'No, Petros didn't tell me. He probably didn't want to worry me. I wouldn't read anything into it if I were you.'

'No?' He smiled thinly, his deep brown eyes reflecting his scepticism. 'So the fact that Petros didn't choose to tell you the truth doesn't upset you, Miss Carlyon?'

'Not at all,' she said rather too quickly. 'Anyway, whatever the reason was for his suspension, it can't have been anything really serious or he would never have been chosen to go on the exchange programme.'

Christos didn't say anything. He still wasn't comfortable

with the part he'd played in that decision. He had pulled a lot of strings to get his cousin the job overseas and had met with a lot of opposition too.

It wasn't that Petros couldn't do the job. If he'd set his mind to it, he could have been a first-rate surgeon. However, Petros preferred to spend his time enjoying himself rather than working, and it was that lack of commitment that had caused the problem.

Petros had left the hospital before a patient had regained consciousness following surgery. He had been unavailable when a problem had arisen and the lapse could have cost the man his life and had almost cost Petros his job. It was only because Christos had pleaded his case that he had been allowed to return to the surgical department, but it was time his cousin knuckled down and paid more attention to his career now he was about to get married.

'You met my cousin while he was working in Manchester, I assume?' Christos deliberately changed the subject. It certainly wouldn't help to dwell on the thought that it was his own over-developed work ethos that had ruined his chances of winning Eleni's heart all those years ago.

'That's right. I was working in A and E and members of the surgical team were always popping into the department. Petros was always so charming whenever we had to call him in, unlike a lot of the other registrars who made it appear as though they were doing us a favour.'

She laughed softly and Christos felt a jolt run through him when he heard the amusement in her voice. For some reason it lifted his own spirits and it took him a moment to recover his composure.

'So it was my cousin's charm you fell for?'

'Amongst other things—yes.' She turned to look at him.

'As I told you on the phone, Dr Constantine, it was Petros who pursued me.'

'Indeed you did. You prefer to play hard to get, do you, Miss Carlyon?'

'No. I prefer not rush into a situation without considering the pros and cons first. It was a while before I agreed to go out with Petros, in fact.'

'Ah, I see. Now I understand.'

'Understand what exactly?'

'The pros of accepting an invitation to go out with Petros, of course. What was the biggest incentive? Was it the fact that his family is extremely wealthy that helped you make up your mind?'

'No! I knew nothing about Petros's family when I agreed to go out with him.'

'Of course not,' he agreed gravely, his tone making a mockery of the claim. Out of the corner of his eye he saw her open her mouth to say something else until she thought better of it. As he turned in through the gates of the hospital, he found himself wondering what she'd been going to say. Had it been another protestation of her innocence, perhaps?

In a way he wished that she had argued with him because then it would have been so much easier to shoot her down. He could have dealt with her anger far better than he could deal with the unhappiness he could see on her face. Maybe Katie Carlyon deserved her comeuppance after the way she had behaved, but he couldn't derive any pleasure from her discomfort. All he felt was a deep sadness that a woman as beautiful as this should use her beauty to such ugly ends. With her soft blonde hair curling around her face and her green eyes dulled with pain, she really did look like an angel—one who had fallen from grace.

Katie could feel tears welling in her eyes and quickly blinked them away. She wouldn't give Dr Constantine the satisfaction of knowing that he had hurt her. Oh, she knew that he had done it deliberately but even that didn't take the sting out of those horrible words. She wasn't interested in Petros's money! It was Petros she loved, not what he could give her.

She had barely managed to get her emotions under control when the car stopped. Christos switched off the engine and turned to her. 'I need to check with my registrar to see how our patient is doing. I suggest you wait in my office and we can talk after I've finished.'

'I really can't see what we have to talk about,' Katie said bluntly as she opened the car door. 'This problem has nothing to do with you, as I told you on the phone.'

'And as I told you, that's where you're wrong.' He turned to look at her and she shivered when she saw the chill in his eyes. 'Petros enlisted my help and I have every intention of doing what I promised him I would do.'

'And what exactly did you promise him?' she said sharply, her heart aching at the thought of Petros asking him to intervene, if, indeed, that was what had happened. She only had Christos's word for it and there was no reason why she should believe him.

'I promised him that I would make sure you didn't cause any trouble. He and Eleni are looking forward to their wedding and I won't allow you to ruin the occasion for them.' He got out of the car and waited until she got out as well. 'I'll take you straight to my office and I expect you to stay there. If you are harbouring any hopes of trying to find Petros while you're here, you can forget them. He's on leave until after his honeymoon is over.'

Katie didn't know what to say. Was it really true, then? Was Petros *really* getting married? She didn't want to believe it yet she couldn't imagine why Christos would have made up such an elaborate story.

In silence she followed him into the building. The hospital was obviously brand-new; everywhere was gleaming with fresh paint. Wide corridors fanned out from the main foyer like the spokes of an enormous wheel, the huge tinted-glass windows that ran along them giving glimpses of the grounds. It was a world away from the grimness of the inner-city hospital where she'd worked so that it was hard to take it all in. However, it was when they reached the trauma unit that the real differences immediately became apparent.

Katie stopped and stared around in genuine wonder. 'I've never seen such marvellous facilities. Is that for the radiography equipment?' she asked, pointing to the tracks running along the ceiling.

'Yes.' Christos stopped as well. 'We have a dedicated radiography unit attached to the department, along with our own theatre suite plus a haematology lab.' He shrugged when she gasped. 'It means we're virtually self-sufficient.'

'It must be wonderful not to have to go begging to other departments for help.' She sighed. 'The number of times I've had to go, cap in hand, to the surgical department doesn't bear thinking about. Just getting a slot in Theatre is a minor miracle some days.'

He smiled faintly. 'I've done my share of begging, too. That's why I insisted on us having our own theatre when the plans were drawn up. It's made a huge difference, not only for the patients but for the staff as well. Morale is higher than it's ever been.'

'I can imagine,' she agreed wistfully as they carried on. They came to the nursing station and she waited while he spoke to the nurse on duty. She could see a row of cubicles on her left and swing doors leading to the resuscitation area on her right. There were other doors leading off from the reception area and she could only assume that they must lead to the various departments he'd mentioned.

She had to admit that she was impressed by what she'd seen. In fact, if circumstances had been different, she would have had no hesitation in applying for a position here. However, she doubted if Dr Constantine would be keen to have her on his team. From what he had said, he seemed to have a very low opinion of her.

The thought was deeply upsetting. Normally, she got on well with people and it was a strange feeling to know that this man disliked her so much. It was difficult to hide how hurtful she found it to be on the receiving end of his animosity when he turned to her.

'There's been a problem with the patient we resuscitated at the airport. He's had a second MI and my registrar is having trouble stabilising him. I don't have time to take you to my office right now so can you wait here?'

'Of course,' Katie agreed, because she could tell he was anxious to attend to the old man. She looked around after he left, wondering where would be the best place to wait. She could see a sign pointing to the waiting room but before she could head towards it the nurse intervened.

'The relatives' room is through there,' she explained, pointing to a door opposite the desk. 'You'll be more comfortable in there than in the waiting room, plus there's tea and coffee in there so help yourself.'

'Thank you.'

Katie quickly moved away from the desk when she saw the curiosity on the other woman's face. The nurse was obviously wondering who she was and she doubted if Christos would appreciate it if she told her. She had a feeling that the less people who knew what she was doing there, the better he would like it.

Despair welled up inside her again. She had no idea what she was going to do if it turned out that he had been telling her the truth. When she had left England that morning, she had left behind everything to do with her old life. Once she and Kelly had decided to move abroad they had given up the lease on their flat and sold all their furniture. There was nothing left in England to go back for now, not even her sister.

Katie felt a lump come to her throat as she checked her watch. Kelly's flight had been due to leave after hers but she would be on her way to Sardinia by now. Kelly had been through a lot in the past two years and a new job was what she needed to put her life back on track. But if she went back to England then Kelly might feel that she had to go back too. Was that really what she wanted? Did she want to spoil Kelly's chance of finding happiness because her own plans hadn't worked out the way she'd hoped they would?

Katie took a deep breath then pushed open the waiting-room door. No matter what happened, she wasn't going back to England. And if that didn't please Dr Christos Constantine, it was hard luck.

'Sinus rhythm,' the nurse announced.

Christos nodded. 'Good. I didn't think we were going to get him back at one point.' He turned to Yanni. 'He's going to need bypass surgery urgently. There are at least three separate sites where the arteries are almost completely blocked. I'd like Alexis to assess him so can you give him a call, please?'

'You're recommending that he has the surgery here rather than at home in England?' Yanni asked.

'Yes. I don't think he would survive the flight home and I am not prepared to take the risk.' He shrugged. 'His insurance should cover the costs, but if there's a problem then we shall do it as an emergency procedure. I'll speak to his wife while you sort things out with the surgical team.'

'Of course.'

Stripping off his gloves, Christos left Resus. Once he had spoken to the patient's wife, he would be able to get on with the business of sorting out this other mess. The only viable solution he could see was to send Katie Carlyon back to England. If she stayed in Paphos there was always the chance of her running into Petros. Although his cousin had claimed that Katie had been hounding him, Christos didn't doubt that he had been happy to spend time with her in the beginning. Katie Carlyon was a very beautiful woman and few men would be able to resist her allure.

Christos wasn't sure why it bothered him to think about all the men who must have passed through Katie Carlyon's life. He tried to put it out of his mind as he made his way to the nursing station to collect her. There was no sign of her when he got there and he frowned.

'If you're looking for the young woman who came in with you, she's in the relatives' room,' Maria, the nurse, informed him. She smiled archly at him. 'Is there something you want to tell me, Christos?'

'No, thank you.' Christos knew what Maria was really asking. She wanted to know if he was romantically involved

with Miss Carlyon. It never failed to amaze him how interested in his affairs—or rather the lack of them—his staff
appeared to be.

He sighed as he made his way to the relatives' room. The
fact that he had taken time off work then reappeared with a
beautiful young woman in tow was bound to excite a lot of
speculation. It was his own fault, of course, for not giving his
staff anything better to talk about, but he couldn't help it if he
rarely dated. He'd been too busy with his work to worry about
his private life. He'd also learned his lesson after what had
happened between him and Eleni. If he hadn't been able to
make a go of it with Eleni, what hope did he have of sustain-
ing a relationship with anyone else?

It was easier if he accepted that he would remain single.
Maybe once upon a time he had dreamed of having a family
of his own, but the likelihood of that happening now was virtually nil. He would need to invest a lot of time and a lot of
effort into a marriage and he wasn't sure if he could do it if
it meant his career would suffer. It was far more sensible to
settle for what he had.

Pushing open the door, he stepped into the room then
stopped dead when he spotted Katie sitting next to his
patient's wife. As he watched, she put her arm around the old
lady's shoulders and hugged her. Christos frowned. There
was such compassion in the gesture that it made all his pre-
conceived ideas about her seem ludicrous. He simply couldn't
equate this kind and caring woman with the manipulative
harridan whom Petros had described at such length.

Which was the real Katie Carlyon? All of a sudden, he
realised that he needed to find out the answer to that question
even though he wasn't sure why it mattered so much.

CHAPTER THREE

'I'M SURE there will be some news soon. Try not to worry.'

Katie hugged the old lady again, wishing there was something more she could say to reassure her. She glanced round when she heard the door slam and flushed when she saw Christos coming towards them. He stopped in front of them and her heart skipped a beat when she saw the look he gave her. Why did she have the strangest feeling that he was studying her?

'Mrs Briggs? I'm Dr Constantine, the head of the trauma unit.'

He pulled up a chair and sat down, his expression softening when he saw the fear on the old lady's face. 'Your husband is alive, Mrs Briggs. He had a second heart attack but we managed to stabilise him. You'll be able to see him very soon.'

'Oh, thank heavens!' Marjorie Briggs clutched Katie's hand. 'I thought you were going to tell me that Frank was dead. I couldn't have stood that, really, I couldn't.'

She broke into a storm of weeping again. Katie patted her hand as she waited for her to calm down. Dealing with distraught relatives had been part of her job for so long that it was second nature to her now. Reaching into her bag, she plucked out a tissue and handed it to her.

'I know it's been a terrible shock for you, Marjorie, but the fact that Frank has rallied for a second time is a really positive sign, isn't it, Dr Constantine?' She glanced at Christos and once again was struck by the feeling that he was assessing her every word and action.

'Indeed it is. Your husband is doing extremely well in the circumstances. However, the next few hours will be critical, you understand.'

'You mean that Frank could have another heart attack?' Marjorie said, her voice quavering.

'Sadly, yes.'

He leant forward and Katie was surprised when she saw real compassion in his eyes. From her experiences that day, she wouldn't have put him down as someone who empathised with other people, but it seemed that she might have misjudged him.

'We've carried out various tests on your husband and established that the cardiac arteries are almost completely blocked in three separate places. I feel it would be safer if he underwent immediate bypass surgery.'

'You mean you want to operate on Frank *here*?' Marjorie exclaimed in dismay.

'Yes. In my opinion it would be far too dangerous to allow him to fly home to England for the operation. We have the facilities to do it here and your travel insurance should cover the cost of the operation plus the aftercare. If it doesn't, then we do have funding available in special cases. All I need is for you to sign a consent form so the operation can go ahead.'

'Oh, I don't know what to do! Frank's never had a day's illness in his life so are you absolutely sure this is necessary?' Marjorie pleaded.

It was obvious the poor woman was overwhelmed by thought of having to make the decision all by herself so Katie gently intervened. 'Dr Constantine wouldn't have suggested it if it weren't in your husband's best interests, Marjorie.'

'Do you really think so?' Marjorie said desperately, turning to her.

'Of course I do,' Katie assured her. 'And if you're worried about Frank having the operation here rather than at home, don't be. I've only seen a small part of the hospital so far, but I have to say that I'm very impressed. The facilities here are excellent.'

'Well, if you think it's the right thing to do, dear.' Marjorie was obviously wavering.

'I do.' Katie smiled encouragingly at her. 'Having the surgery here will give your husband the best possible chance of making a full recovery.'

'Then that's what we'll do.' Marjorie took a deep breath and stood up. 'I'll sign whatever forms you need, Doctor. Then I'd like to see my husband, please.'

'Of course.' Christos stood up as well. Putting his hand under the old lady's elbow, he guided her to the door then paused. 'I shall only be a few minutes if you wouldn't mind waiting here for me.'

'Of course.'

Katie stood up after they left and went to the window. It was a beautiful day, the sun beating down from a cloudless blue sky. She could see right across the bay and the reflection of the sun glittering off the aquamarine water would have been breathtaking at any other time. However, she found it impossible to derive any pleasure from the view right then. She might have helped to solve Marjorie's problem but she still hadn't solved her own. What on earth was she going to do if it turned out that Petros really was getting married? Should she stay in Cyprus when the plans she'd made for the future would never amount to anything, or should she leave the island? And if she left, where should she go?

She could go to Sardinia and join Kelly, but that might put a damper on her sister's plans. Knowing Kelly, she would throw herself into her new job and soon make lots of friends. Having her twin around might hold her back, though, and that was the last thing Katie wanted to do, yet the thought of moving to another country on her own was a daunting one.

She didn't have Kelly's confidence and couldn't imagine making a life for herself in a place where she knew nobody so she might be forced to return to England after all. However, the prospect of going back to Manchester wasn't one she relished. All her friends and workmates knew why she had left and the thought of having to tell them about Petros was more than she could bear. She certainly didn't want to become an object of pity!

She was still trying to work out what she should do for the best when the door opened and her heart sank when she realised that Christos had returned. She knew that he would want her to leave as soon as possible, but was she prepared to go without seeing Petros first? Maybe Christos had told her the truth, but she needed to hear it from Petros himself rather than from a go-between. No matter where she ended up, she knew that she would never be able to settle until she had resolved this issue.

Christos could tell as soon as he went back into the room that he was going to have a fight on his hands if he hoped to persuade Katie to leave. There was a glint in her eyes that didn't bode well for any plans he might harbour. He decided to opt for the gentle approach and smiled at her.

'Shall we go up to my office? It will be quieter there and there will be less chance of us being interrupted.'

He opened the door but she ignored his invitation. Walking over to the chairs, she picked up her bag. 'I don't think so. The only place I'm going is into the town to find myself a room for the night.'

'Why? What point is there in staying here?' He shrugged, trying to stave off a sudden feeling of disappointment. Maybe he did want to learn more about her but he couldn't afford to satisfy his curiosity at the expense of Eleni's happiness. The longer Katie remained on the island, the greater the risk of Eleni finding out about her and that was the last thing he wanted. 'The best thing you can do now is to return to England and put this whole unfortunate episode behind you.'

'Whether I return to England or not is my decision. I don't need you to tell me what to do.' She marched to the door, one slender brow arching when he barred her way. 'Excuse me.'

'You aren't going anywhere until I know what you intend to do.'

'Really?' She stared up at him, her pretty face set. 'Holding me here against my will is a crime, Dr Constantine. Are you prepared for the publicity that will follow if I report you to the police?'

'The police would never believe you,' he scoffed, hoping he was right.

'Maybe not, but they would have to investigate my allegations.' She smiled tightly. 'These things have a nasty habit of leaking out. I wonder how Petros's fiancée will feel if she sees the story plastered across the front of the local paper.'

Christos knew that she was calling his bluff but there was little he could do about it. She was right, too, because the papers would have a field day if the story got out. Both Petros's and Eleni's families were well known on the island and anything that involved them was big news. He couldn't bear to imagine how devastated Eleni would be if the papers printed the whole sorry tale.

He stepped aside, knowing that he couldn't take that risk. He would have to find another way to ensure Katie's co-operation, although it wasn't going to be easy. She was a very determined young woman, it seemed.

He followed her from the room, wondering how he should handle the situation from here on. Maria was still working behind the desk; she looked up when he and Katie passed.

'You haven't introduced me to your friend yet, Christos,' she chided him.

'I'm sorry.' Christos stopped, knowing it would create more speculation if he ignored her. 'This is Katie Carlyon, Maria. She was at the airport when Mr Briggs collapsed and she helped to resuscitate him.'

'*Kalimera*, Katie.' Maria smiled warmly. 'You were very brave to lend a hand. It can be quite scary when you have to resuscitate someone like that.'

'It certainly can.' Katie returned her smile. 'Fortunately, I'm an emergency department nurse so I've done my share of CPR over the years.'

'It was lucky you were there!' Maria exclaimed. 'So what brings you to our beautiful island? Are you here on holiday?'

'Not really. I was supposed to be moving here to live, but my plans might have to change. I'm not sure what I'm going to do now, to be honest.'

Christos could tell that Maria was dying to know what had happened to change Katie's plans and hurriedly intervened. There was no way that he wanted Katie to discuss the situation with a member of his staff. Gossip was rife in the hospital and it wouldn't take long for the story to circulate throughout the building and beyond.

'I don't want to rush you, Katie, but if you're hoping to find somewhere to stay tonight, you'd better not leave it too late. The hotels soon get booked up as more flights arrive.' He grasped her arm and steered her towards the corridor, waiting until they were out of Maria's sight before he released her.

'Do you mind?' She glared at him as she rubbed her arm. 'I would prefer it if you didn't manhandle me.'

'And I would prefer it if you saw sense and got on a plane back to England.' He returned her stare, knowing that he had to convince her it was a waste of time remaining on the island. 'I don't know what you hope to achieve by staying here. I've already explained the situation to you, but in case you're in any doubt, Petros isn't interested in you. Is that clear?'

'Yes, thank you—perfectly clear.' Tears sparkled in her eyes but she blinked them away. 'However, until Petros tells me that himself then I am not leaving. For all I know you could be making it up.'

He swore softly in Greek, glad that she couldn't understand the ugly words. It was rare that he lost his temper but she had pushed him to the limit that day. 'Why would I make it up? What possible reason could I have for doing so? I'm telling you the truth, Katie, so do yourself a favour and accept it.'

'I can't.' Her voice was so low that he had to strain to hear what she was saying. 'I wish I could walk away but I can't until I hear Petros say that he doesn't love me.'

Her voice broke as tears began to stream down her face. Christos wasn't sure if it was the sight of those tears that affected him, but there wasn't a doubt in his mind at that moment that she was suffering and he responded instinctively. Gathering her into his arms, he rocked her gently to and fro. He understood how devastated she must feel because it was how he had felt when he'd lost Eleni. The worst kind of pain was that which came from knowing that you could never have the person you loved most of all.

In that moment his feelings towards Katie suddenly shifted. He could no longer think of her simply as a problem to be solved as speedily as possible. She was suffering, too, and knowing that forged a bond between them he had never anticipated. He realised with a sinking heart that it was going to be harder than he'd imagined to fulfil his promise to his cousin and send her away.

Katie could feel the warm strength of the arms that were holding her and for the first time in ages she felt safe. She hadn't realised until then how stressful the past few weeks had been. Leaving England and everything she knew had been a huge step. Even though she'd been sure it was what she'd wanted to do, it had been a major decision for her. If she'd had any idea this would happen then she would never have got on the plane that morning, but it was too late for regrets now. She had to deal with the situation as best she could, and learn from it.

'Here.'

A large tanned hand suddenly appeared in front of her, holding a crisp white handkerchief. Katie took it with a murmur of thanks and dried her eyes. When Christos let her go, she forced herself to smile at him even though there was very little to smile about. 'Thank you.'

'Feeling better now?' he asked quietly.

'Yes. I'm sorry. I don't usually go to pieces like that.'

'There's no need to apologise. You're upset and I understand why.' He sighed. 'That's why I think it would be best if you went home.'

'I'm not sure what I want to do,' she admitted. 'This has been a huge shock and I need time to think before I make any decisions.'

'Surely it would be easier to do that in England with your family and friends around you.'

'The only family I have is my sister Kelly and she's in Sardinia. She flew out there this morning to take up a new job and I certainly don't want to upset her plans by telling her that things haven't worked out for me.'

'I see. But what about your friends? There must be people who you are close to?'

'Yes.' She shrugged. 'I have some really good friends back in Manchester but they have their own problems. It isn't fair to expect them to help me.'

'So what you're saying is that you don't want to return to England?'

'I don't know! My head's in such a spin that I don't know what I want to do. That's why I need time to think things through. I certainly don't want to go rushing into another decision I'll regret.'

She brushed past him because there was no point debating the issue any more. Anyway, he didn't really care where she went so long as it was away from the island, and far away from Petros.

A sob rose to her throat but she forced it down. They had reached the foyer and she paused. 'I'll find a taxi to take me into town. If you could fetch my case out of your car, I'll be out of your way in no time.'

'And what about Petros? Do you still intend to contact him?'

'Of course. However, I shall decide when and how I intend to do so. It has nothing to do with you or anyone else.'

'That isn't good enough, I'm afraid. You have to understand the damage you could cause.'

'What about the damage that has been done to me?' she countered, angrily. 'Doesn't that count for anything?'

'Of course it does, which is why I want you to be sensible and forget about my cousin. He isn't right for you, Katie. Can't you see that?'

'At the moment I'm too confused to know what I think any more,' she said wearily.

'I understand, but promise me that you won't do anything rash.'

He captured her hands and held them fast, and once again she was struck by a feeling of security. It was very strange because nothing he had said to her that day should have made her feel like this, yet it didn't alter the fact that she felt safer with him then she'd felt with anyone, even Petros.

The thought shocked her so much that she snatched her hands away. 'I won't make promises I might not be able to keep.'

He shook his head in despair. 'I don't know what else I can say to convince you.'

'There's nothing you can say. I need to make up my own mind.'

'And what will you do in the meantime? Are you going to treat this as a holiday?'

'I'm not sure.' Katie sighed because that was something else she needed to think about. The money she had left after paying for her flight wouldn't last long if she had to stay in a hotel. She might be able to find somewhere cheaper—a guest house or maybe a room—but even then it wouldn't be long before her money ran out. She hadn't given any thought to her financial position before she'd left England. She had assumed that Petros would ask her to live with him but that wasn't going to happen now.

Pain lanced through her again. She had trusted Petros and he had let her down. Although it wouldn't change what had happened, she needed to know why he had treated her this way. And to do that she would have to find a way to support herself so she could remain on the island.

'I could manage a week's holiday, but I'll need to find a job after that. I can't afford to stay on here if I'm not earning any money.'

'It might not be that easy to find work.' He shrugged when she looked at him in surprise. 'It's still quite early in the season and a lot of the restaurants and bars aren't taking on extra staff yet.'

'I'm sure I'll find something,' she said, wondering if this was another ploy to put her off the idea of staying on the island.

He sighed. 'I am not making it up, Katie. I'm merely explaining the problems you could encounter.'

'Thank you for your concern, but I'm sure I'll find myself some sort of a job,' she said shortly.

'You said that you were a nurse in the emergency department—is that right?'

'Yes. I was a senior staff nurse in Accident and Emergency. Why? Do you have a vacancy on your team?'

The question was asked very much with her tongue in her cheek. She didn't seriously think that he would consider hiring her, even if there was a vacancy, so it was impossible to hide her surprise when he said quietly, 'We do have a vacancy, as it happens. If your references check out then I can see no reason why I shouldn't offer you the job.' He smiled thinly when she gasped. 'Please, don't misunderstand why I'm doing this, though. I haven't changed my mind about you staying on here. I still believe that you should go home. But we are in desperate need of staff, and if you are intent on staying here, you may as well help us out.'

CHAPTER FOUR

'THIS is Yanni, one of our senior registrars. And Tina and Ariadne, who are both nurses. Oh, and that's Takis over there— he's the radiographer. OK, everyone, this is Katie Carlyon.'

'*Kalimera*, Katie!'

'*Kalimera!*' Katie responded as everyone chorused a greeting. It was her first day at work in the trauma unit and she was still finding it hard to believe that she was actually there. However, as Christos had predicted, there had been very little other work available. She had soon realised that if she wanted to remain on the island, she would have to accept his offer. She'd felt incredibly nervous when she'd arrived, but Maria had quickly put her at her ease by introducing her to the rest of the staff. Fortunately everyone wore a name badge so that should help her to avoid any embarrassing lapses of memory.

'That is enough for now. You can meet the others later.' Maria linked her arm through Katie's and briskly led her to the staffroom. 'We shall have a cup of coffee while you tell me all about your relationship with Christos.'

'My relationship with Christos?' Katie echoed in bemusement.

'*Ne*.' Maria laughed. 'Oh, I am not asking you to be indiscreet but it was obvious the other day that you and Christos were...*friends.*'

Katie blushed. The tone of Maria's voice had put a whole new spin on the word. 'Oh, no, you've got it wrong,' she said quickly. 'Christos and I only met the other day at the airport. There's nothing going on between us, I assure you.'

'*Óhi?*' Maria looked sceptical. 'But it was Christos who arranged for you to have this job, wasn't it?'

'Yes, but only because I happened to mention that I'd worked in an emergency department in the UK.' She shrugged, doing her best to deflect Maria's suspicions. It certainly wouldn't improve Christos's opinion of her if she was the cause of any unsavoury gossip.

She wasn't sure why it should matter what he thought of her, and hurried on. 'I expect it was easier to offer me the job than go through all the rigmarole of finding someone else.'

'I see.' Maria didn't appear wholly convinced but before she could question her further, the wail of a siren warned them that there was an ambulance on its way.

Katie hurriedly followed her to the doors that led to the ambulance bay and waited while the crew unloaded the stretcher. She grabbed hold of the saline drip as the convoy swept towards Resus. Fortunately, English was widely used in the hospital and she had no difficulty following what was said as the paramedics explained that the young man had been injured while he'd been parasailing at a resort further along the coast. By the time they finished detailing the patient's obs and the treatment he'd received, she was fully up to speed.

'So, what do we have?' Christos arrived just as they were about to transfer the patient onto a bed. He glanced at Katie,

obviously expecting her to answer. Maybe it was meant to be
a test of her skills but she didn't waste time worrying about it.

'Simon Bradshaw, aged nineteen, injured when his para-
chute collapsed while he was parasailing.' She grasped a
corner of the spinal board, keeping up a flow of information
about the young man's pulse, BP and sats levels as they moved
him across to the bed. 'Possible spinal injuries, plus injuries
to his left leg and foot.'

'Was he conscious when the crew got to him?' Christos
demanded.

'Yes. The pilot of the speedboat told the paramedics that
he was conscious and breathing when they pulled him out of
the water.'

'Good.' He bent over the young man. 'My name is Christos
Constantine and I'm the head of the trauma unit. I need to
assess the extent of your injuries, especially any damage that
has been done to your spine, so I'm going to have to leave you
on this board for a while longer. OK?'

'Yes.' The young man groaned. 'My left leg is killing me.
And my right arm doesn't feel too clever either.'

'Good. The fact that you can feel pain in those areas means
there's a strong chance you haven't damaged your spinal
cord,' Christos said calmly. 'I'll give you something for the
pain after I've finished examining you.'

Katie moved aside as he bent over and shone a light into
the patient's eyes. He was blocking her path so she stayed
where she was until he finished. He was so close to her that
she could see that there wasn't a trace of silver in his thick
black hair, and frowned.

How old was he? she wondered suddenly. He exuded such
an air of authority that she'd assumed he must be a lot older

than Petros, but from what she could tell he could be only in his late thirties. Petros was thirty-two so there wasn't that big of an age gap between them. However, Petros definitely didn't inspire the same degree of confidence that his cousin did.

It felt strange to find herself comparing the two men, and stranger still to realise that Petros had come off worst. As Christos moved away, she felt a little pang run through her. It was understandable that her feelings towards Petros should have changed after what had happened, but if she'd loved him as much as she'd thought she'd done then surely she should have remained true to him? Real love was supposed to last for ever; it wasn't supposed to fade as soon as it encountered an obstacle. However, she couldn't put her hand on her heart and swear that she loved him as much as she'd done when they'd been in England. It made her wonder if there could be any guarantees where love was concerned.

'There's some swelling over the cervical spine. I'd like another X-ray of the area, please.'

Christos glanced over his shoulder to check the Takis had heard him and frowned when he saw the expression on Katie's face. He had no idea what was going through her mind at that moment but he didn't think he'd seen anyone who looked so lost before. He cleared his throat, not wanting her to suspect how much it had unsettled him.

'I need another litre of saline, Katie. And a second line put in, please.'

He turned away as she hurried off to carry out his instructions. Fortunately, the beds in Resus were multi-functional; there was no need to move the patient to get the shots he wanted. He reviewed his findings while Takis organised the X-rays.

The first set of films had confirmed that Simon Bradshaw had a fractured left tibia as well as a serious fracture of the left calcaneus, or heel bone. There was compression of the bone which could cause permanent damage to the joints involved in turning the foot in and out, and create problems walking. Christos made a note to ask his colleagues in Orthopaedics to review the X-rays before the patient left Resus, but at the moment he was more concerned about the possibility of spinal damage. Fortunately, the radiography equipment was linked to a sophisticated computer system and it took only minutes before the images were ready to be displayed on the screen.

'It looks as though one of the discs in the cervical spine has ruptured.' He pointed to the area in question as Yanni came to join him. 'See how the prolapsed disc is protruding into the spinal cord. It's compressing the root of the nerve leading to the arm.'

'Do you think it will it need surgery to repair it?' Yanni asked.

'There's no way of knowing at this stage,' Christos replied. 'We shall have to wait until the swelling subsides before a decision is made.'

He left Yanni still studying the films and went back to the bed. Katie had returned and he nodded when she asked him if she should set up the second drip. At least she seemed more in control of herself now, he thought in relief, then wondered why he had been so worried about her.

'So what's the damage, Doctor? Am I going to live?'

'Yes.' Christos smiled at the young man. Despite Simon's apparently upbeat attitude, Christos could tell that he was anxious about the prognosis. He immediately set about reas-suring him. 'Your injuries are definitely not life-threatening, although you aren't in the clear just yet. The X-rays have shown that one of the discs in your cervical spine has ruptured.'

'My cervical spine… Sorry, but I was never that good at biology when I was at school. Could you explain what you mean?'

'The cervical spine is the top part of your backbone. It's made up of seven vertebrae—they're the knobbly bits of bone that protect your spinal cord—and the very top one supports your head. In between each of the vertebrae is a disc that consists of a hard outer layer and a jelly-like core. These discs act as shock absorbers and cushion the vertebrae when you move your spine.'

'And it's one of these discs that's damaged?'

'That's right. When you landed in the water, you must have twisted your spine and part of the pulpy core of the disc got squeezed out. It's compressing the nerve that leads to your arm.'

'Which is why it feels all sort of numb and tingly,' Simon concluded.

'Exactly. Your neck will probably feel stiff as well, although you probably haven't noticed it because the head restraints are restricting your movements.'

'So what happens now?' Simon grimaced. 'You can repair this disc, can't you?'

'It could very well repair itself once the swelling has gone down. We shall have to wait and see. However, I have to warn you that it could be a long process and you will need to be patient. The treatment for this type of injury is total bed rest.'

'Oh, great! You mean I'm going to be flat on my back for the next few weeks?' Simon groaned. 'We only arrived yesterday, too. It looks as though that's put paid to my holiday, doesn't it?'

'Count yourself lucky,' Christos admonished. 'The situation could have been a lot worse if you'd damaged your spinal cord.'

Simon obviously saw the sense of that although he still looked glum. Christos asked Tina to contact the orthopaedic surgeon as well as the spinal unit. Although he hadn't told the patient about the long-term implications of injuring his foot, it would need to be dealt with, too. All things considered this wasn't going to be the kind of holiday the young man had hoped for and he could understand his disappointment.

He glanced round when he heard Katie ask Maria what she should do next. Here was someone else who had suffered a major disappointment since she'd arrived on the island. Just for a moment he found himself wishing that he hadn't been so hard on her before he realised what he was doing. He couldn't afford to sympathise with Katie in case he lost sight of the main issue.

Katie knew that Christos was watching her but she didn't look round. He had made no secret of his reasons for offering her this job and she was under no illusions. He wanted her there so he could keep an eye on her.

She cleared away the soiled dressings and put them in the bio-hazard sack. Tina was busy making phone calls and Maria had been called away to deal with a patient in cubicles. When Simon called out for a nurse, she hurried over to him.

'It won't be long before you're moved out of here,' she assured him. 'We're just waiting for the orthopaedic surgeon to look at your leg and your foot first.'

'That's what I'm worried about. I didn't bother buying any travel insurance before I came away, so I don't know how I'm going to pay for all this. It was another thirty pounds and me and my mates couldn't see the point of spending all that money on something we weren't going to use.'

Katie sighed. 'Nobody can foretell when an accident is going to happen.'

'That's what my mum said.' Simon groaned. 'Mum will go mad when she finds out what's happened. She said it was asking for trouble if a gang of us went away together but I wouldn't listen to her. I've just finished re-sitting my A levels and I needed a break after all the studying. I've been saving up for ages for this holiday, too, and now I've completely messed up.'

'Don't worry.' Katie patted his arm when tears come to his eyes. 'I'm sure we'll be able to sort something out about the cost of your treatment. In the meantime, do you want me to phone your mum and tell her what's happened?'

'I suppose you'll have to,' Simon said glumly. He gave her his home phone number then the orthopaedic surgeon arrived. In the end it was decided that Simon needed to go straight to Theatre to have his leg set and to repair the damage to his heel. He would be taken to the spinal care unit once that was done.

Katie saw him off then went to the nursing station and explained to Maria that she needed to make a phone call to England. She told Simon's mother what had happened, and reassured her as best she could that Simon was in no immediate danger. Christos was just leaving Resus by the time she finished the call so she hurried after him and explained about the young man's lack of medical insurance.

'It happens more times than I can count,' he said wearily. 'People assume they won't need insurance because nothing is going to happen to them. Sadly, they're more likely to have an accident while they're on holiday than they are when they're at home.'

'Being out of your comfort zone makes you do all sorts of crazy things,' she said softly.

'It does. Even the most sensible people take unacceptable risks.' He shrugged. 'We have a system in Cyprus that provides emergency care for any visitors to the island so leave it with me. Thank you for letting me know, Katie.'

'You're welcome.' She smiled at him, wondering why a few polite words should have lifted her spirits. Was it the fact that she knew up until now he had regarded her as nothing more than a nuisance?

She sighed as he hurried away. She really couldn't blame him after what Petros had said about her, but it still rankled. It made her see how important it was that she clear her name, although she had no idea how she was going to make Petros admit that he'd lied about her. She'd been on the island for over a week now and he still hadn't contacted her. A couple of times she had been tempted to phone him but she had resisted. She didn't want to give him any more reason to accuse her of harassing him so she would bide her time until the moment was right. She also didn't want to be responsible for ruining another woman's life, although maybe it would have made more sense to warn Eleni what her future husband was like.

She grimaced because she could imagine Christos's reaction if she did that. He would probably have her deported from the island—in chains!

It was a busy day and Katie was surprised by the number of people they treated. Any thoughts she'd had about the delights of working in such a beautiful place as Cyprus soon disappeared. People still got sick and injured themselves no matter how brightly the sun shone. By the time her shift ended, she was looking forward to going home. She'd managed to find herself a room above a café in the town centre. It was basic but clean, and much cheaper than staying in a hotel. She caught the bus outside the hospital and was home in less than half an hour.

Normally she cooked a meal for herself, but she felt too tired to bother that night. She decided to eat out as a treat so once she had showered and changed, she headed down to the harbour. There were plenty of bars and restaurants there, although she didn't stop immediately but carried on until she reached the fort at the end of the harbour wall. It felt good to be outside after being indoors all day and she might as well make the most of it.

She sat down on the wall and watched the pelicans swooping across the bay as they searched for fish. The air was still very warm even though the daylight was fading. The sun was dropping lower in the sky, casting fingers of brilliant red and orange light across the water. The smell of fresh herbs and olive oil wafted towards her from the nearby restaurants and she sniffed appreciatively. There were a lot of people about—couples strolling arm in arm, young families with children in pushchairs—and they all seemed to be enjoying the evening in each other's company.

Katie felt a lump suddenly come to her throat. She should have been sitting here tonight with Petros. *They* should have been enjoying the evening together. How could he have lied to her, made her believe that he loved her when he was engaged to someone else? Had he told her that he loved her because it had been the only way he could get her to sleep with him?

The realization hit her and her eyes filled with tears when she realised how stupid she had been. She had been determined not to make the same mistake her parents had made, but she'd been just as foolish. The thought of eating dinner was suddenly more than she could bear. She just wanted to go back to her room and stay there until all the pain went away.

She scrambled to her feet and hurried back along the path, pushing past a couple who were strolling along in front of her. Tears blinded her so that she didn't even notice the man who was walking towards her until she cannoned right into him. If he hadn't reacted so quickly, in fact, she would have fallen over, but he grasped tight hold of her arms and steadied her.

'Katie? What's the matter? Why are you crying?'

Katie stared up at Christos in shock. She had no idea what he was doing there... Unless he had followed her. Anger suddenly roared through her at the unfairness of it all. She was being treated like a criminal yet she had done nothing wrong!

'Did you follow me here?'

'Of course not. Whatever gave you that idea?'

'The fact that you just *happened* to appear, of course.' She laughed scornfully. 'Please, don't tell me it was coincidence that brought you here tonight, Dr Constantine, because I don't believe you.'

'That is your prerogative, of course,' he said, his eyes boring into hers. 'However, the truth is that I had no idea you would be here—how could I have known? I was still working when your shift ended.'

He sounded sincere enough but Katie refused to be duped again. She'd thought that Petros had been sincere when he'd told her that he'd loved her, and look how that had turned out. 'You could have followed me when I left home.'

'Yes, I suppose I could have done.' He shrugged, his broad shoulders moving lightly under his suit jacket. 'However, as

I was in a meeting until half an hour ago, it would have been difficult for me to get to where you live in time to follow you.'

Katie bit her lip. Although she hated to admit it, it did sound as though he was telling her the truth. He obviously sensed her indecision because he sighed wearily.

'I didn't follow you, Katie. I came down here to have dinner, and that's all.'

'That's why I came, too,' she admitted. 'I thought I'd eat out as a treat.'

'Then why don't we join forces?'

'Join forces?' she queried, not sure what he meant. She stared up at him in confusion and felt her heart lurch when he smiled at her. Now that the stern lines of his face had softened, she realised all of a sudden how handsome he was. With those chiselled features and liquid dark eyes, he was a truly arresting sight and everything that was feminine in her responded to him. She was still trying to deal with that thought when he continued.

'I think we're both adult enough to suspend the hostilities for one evening, don't you, Katie? So will you have dinner with me? Please.'

CHAPTER FIVE

'So, KATIE, what will you have to eat?'

Christos closed the menu, hoping that Katie couldn't tell how on edge he felt. He still wasn't sure why he had asked her to have dinner with him. Maybe it was the fact that she'd looked so upset but he'd known that he couldn't walk away and leave her. It had been the same in Resus that morning when he'd seen her looking so lost: he'd wanted to comfort and protect her then, too, and it was worrying to know how susceptible he was to her moods. He couldn't afford to empathise with her when she could be the cause of so much heartache.

'I can't decide. It all sounds so good that I don't know what to choose.' She smiled shyly at him and once again he found himself responding to her.

'How about the *meze*?' he suggested, doing his best to control the grin that was tilting the corners of his mouth. Maybe he had suggested that they eat together but he mustn't make the mistake of seeing it as anything more than a sensible solution to a problem. She'd been upset and he'd wanted to make sure that she was all right—there'd been no other reason for him issuing the invitation…

Had there?

He cleared his throat, not wanting to go any further down that route. 'If we have the *meze*, you can have a taste of everything on the menu.'

'Sounds good to me so long as you don't think I'm being greedy,' she said with another tiny smile.

'Of course not,' he said firmly, determined to get a grip on himself. 'Anyway, they will be very small portions, like the dishes you get in a tapas bar in Spain.'

'Oh, that's all right, then. Kelly and I went to Seville last year and we had the tapas there. They were lovely.'

'Kelly is your sister?' He leant back in his chair, wondering if this might be the opening he'd been hoping for to find out more about her. It might help him deal with the situation if he understood her better.

'That's right. Kelly and I are twins, fraternal twins, though, not identical ones.' She laughed. 'We're not at all alike. Kelly is tall and slim with the most fabulous red hair. She could have been a model if she'd wanted to. She's so beautiful.'

There was genuine admiration in her voice as she described her sister, and Christos frowned. In his experience it was rare to hear one woman speak so generously about another. It certainly didn't gel with the image Petros had painted of her either. According to his cousin, Katie was a grasping, manipulative woman who put her own interests before everyone else's, although he had to admit that he had seen little sign of it so far.

It was worrying to think that his cousin might have misled him. He tried not to dwell on it because he couldn't afford to start having doubts at this stage. 'What does you sister do? Is she a nurse like you?'

'No, she's a paediatrician. She's really brilliant at her job, too.'

Once again he could hear the pride in her voice and once

again he experienced the same uncomfortable feeling that Petros hadn't been as truthful as he should have been. Christos realised that for his own peace of mind he needed to clarify the situation, not that it would change anything, of course. His cousin was still going to marry Eleni, and he was still going to do everything in his power to ensure that nothing spoiled their special day.

'I see. You mentioned that your sister had moved to Sardinia. Does she intend to carry on with her work there?' he asked, determined not to let Katie know how ambivalent he felt.

'Oh, yes. It's the reason she decided to move there, in fact. Kelly has been offered a job at a new clinic that's recently opened there, you see. They work with children who are seriously ill and they've been achieving some amazing results.' She sighed. 'It's Kelly's dream job and it couldn't have come along at a better time either.'

'Really?' Christos paused as the waiter arrived to take their order. He ordered *meze* for them both, opting for both the fish and the meat dishes. 'Why was it such a propitious time for your sister to take this job?' he asked as soon as the waiter had departed.

'Kelly has been through a really tough time in the past two years. She needed to get away and make a fresh start, although I do miss her. We've never been apart before and it feels very strange, not having her around.'

'Maybe you could move to Sardinia as well.'

Her face immediately closed up. 'I haven't made up my mind what I intend to do.'

Christos sighed. It was obvious that she was determined to remain in Cyprus for the foreseeable future and that it was a bone of contention between them. Fortunately the first few dishes arrived just then. Katie sniffed appreciatively as the waiter finished arranging them on the table.

'Everything smells delicious but what's in them?'

'This dish is slices of *loukanika*—a type of smoked sausage which is very popular in Cyprus. And these are dolmades—vine leaves stuffed with savoury rice.' He pointed to a third dish. 'That's *halloumi* cheese. It's made from goats' milk and usually served grilled with an olive oil and caper dressing.'

'Mmm, it sounds lovely.' Katie scooped a little of everything onto her plate. She sighed as she popped a tiny dolmade into her mouth. 'This is gorgeous!'

Christos laughed, enjoying her delight in the simple food. 'There are a lot more dishes to come,' he warned, piling a couple of dolmades onto his own plate.

'I shall have to pace myself. I'm supposed to be on a diet, although I can't see me sticking to it tonight.'

He smiled at the rueful note in her voice. 'From where I'm sitting, you look beautiful as you are,' he said truthfully.

His gaze skimmed over her, taking stock of the feminine curves of her body. She was wearing a simple cotton sundress that night. The bodice was modestly cut, providing only a glimpse of her full breasts. She'd left her hair loose and the fine blonde strands curled around her bare shoulders like a golden waterfall. Christos felt a sudden tightening in his chest. She looked so young and so lovely that he would have needed a heart of stone not to be aware of her.

'Thank you.'

She accepted the compliment with an easy grace that surprised him. All too often, he'd found that a compliment was met with a denial aimed at eliciting more flattering remarks, but she had accepted what he'd said without any fuss. Was she really as guileless as she appeared to be, or was it all part of an act?

If he was to believe his cousin then he shouldn't have to think about that question. However, it was becoming increasingly difficult to accept that Petros had been telling him the truth and it left him in a quandary. He wouldn't like to think that he was being unfair to Katie, yet he couldn't afford to side with her if it meant there was a chance that Eleni could get hurt.

'*Efcharistó.*' Katie murmured her thanks as the waiter finished arranging a fresh selection of dishes on the table. She leant forward and examined a bowl of some kind of meat stew. 'What's this?' she asked, glancing at Christos. She frowned when she saw the grim expression on his face because it was obvious that there was something troubling him.

'*Kleftiko.* It's made from pieces of lamb that have been cooked very slowly in a special oven.' He made an obvious effort to collect himself and smiled at her. 'Try it. I think you will like it.'

Katie ladled a spoonful onto her plate. The meat was so tender that it fell apart in her mouth. 'It's delicious,' she said, doing her best to behave as though nothing was wrong. Christos had been the perfect host so far and she had enjoyed the evening far more than she had expected to do. However, she mustn't forget that his first allegiance was to his cousin, not her.

The thought was oddly depressing, although she had no idea why. Christos had made his feelings clear from the outset and there was no reason why she should have hoped that he had changed his mind about her. Just because he had invited her to dinner, it didn't mean that he wanted her company. He'd probably only asked her because it had been the perfect way to keep tabs on her.

'Try some of this as well.' He pushed another dish towards her. 'It's kalamari—squid cooked in a light batter.'

'No, thank you. I don't think I can eat anything else.'

Katie placed her knife and fork neatly on her plate. There was a lump in her throat the size of Africa and she couldn't have swallowed another morsel of food. The truth was that Christos didn't give a damn what happened to her so long as she didn't make waves before this wedding took place. What a fool she'd been not to remember that when she'd accepted his invitation to dine with him.

'Are you sure?'

Katie shivered when he subjected her to a searching look. Was he weighing her up again, wondering what she was going to do and how he could stop her? Probably. One thing was certain: he didn't give a damn about her feelings.

'Quite sure,' she said, abruptly pushing back her chair. Opening her bag, she took out some money and placed it on the table. 'That should cover my share of the meal, I think.'

'Surely you aren't leaving so soon,' he protested, rising to his feet. 'How about some coffee if you don't want anything else to eat?'

'Thank you but no. I've had enough and I would like to go home now.' She smiled thinly, wondering why it was so painful to know that he didn't care about her. 'In case you're worried what I might get up to, there's no need. I don't intend to contact Petros tonight. Good night, Dr Constantine. Enjoy the rest of your evening in peace.'

She brushed past the waiter who was in the process of bringing their next selection of dishes and left. Night had fallen now and beyond the harbour wall the sea shimmered like a length of black satin. The scene was exactly how she had imagined it would look. The only difference was that she had pictured herself enjoying the long, hot summer nights with Petros, but that was never going to happen. It wasn't her Petros wanted but some other woman so what was the point of torturing herself? Surely it would be more sensible to leave the island and forget about him?

Katie left the harbour and headed towards the town centre, her mind racing. She would return to England as soon as she could get on a flight home, and once she got there she would find herself another job and somewhere else to live. She wasn't the first woman who'd been let down by a man and she would survive. She would get on with her life and put what had happened behind her.

It would be that easy, would it? a small voice inside her head taunted. She could just expunge all the unhappy memories and carry on as though nothing had happened?

Her footsteps slowed because in her heart she knew it wouldn't be easy at all. Not only did she have to contend with the heartache of losing the man she loved but with the injustice of it. Her reputation had been tarnished by Petros's lies and he should be forced to make amends for what he'd done. Maybe it wouldn't change what had happened but it wasn't fair that people like Christos should carry on thinking that she'd been the instigator of this sorry affair.

Katie took a deep breath. She would leave Cyprus all right, but she wouldn't leave just yet. She intended to clear her name before she left. And once everything was sorted out, she would take great pleasure from making Christos apologise for thinking so badly of her.

* * *

'Can you ask your aunt how she came to injure herself?'

Katie waited while the young woman translated the question for her. The trauma unit had been packed when she'd arrived for work that day. The backlog had been caused by a group of tourists who had been rushed into hospital during the early hours of the morning with food poisoning. Every cubicle was full and there were people in the treatment rooms as well. Maria and Tina were attending to them, leaving her and Ariadne to deal with the other patients. Folding screens had been erected in the waiting area to provide extra examination space, but she would be glad when everything got back to normal.

'My aunt said that she tripped when she was going outside with her washing,' The young woman sighed. 'I keep telling her that I will do her washing for her but she insists on doing all the housework herself.'

'I imagine it's difficult to rely on other people when you're used to being independent,' Katie said, smiling at the old lady.

Theodora Mouskos was eighty-three years old. She had been rushed into hospital with a suspected hip fracture after being found in her garden by a neighbour. She didn't speak English so Katie had been glad when Theodora's great-niece had arrived and offered to translate for her.

'She is far too independent!' the niece declared. 'She refuses to let any of the family help her.'

'Well, if this hip is fractured, I'm afraid she will have to accept your help,' Katie warned her. 'It will be a while before it heals and she won't be able to manage on her own.'

'Then I shall insist that she comes to stay with me,' the niece said firmly.

Katie excused herself and went to find Yanni, thinking how refreshing it was to meet a family member who was so

concerned about an elderly relative. When her father had been
in hospital following his stroke, there had been a number of
old people in the ward who'd not had any visitors. It had been
so sad to see them sitting there, day after day, on their own.

Yanni was just leaving the treatment room with Christos
when she pushed back the screen so she hurried after them.
'Could you take a look at a patient for me, Yanni?' she asked
politely when both men stopped.

'Yanni is dealing with a patient,' Christos explained. 'His
condition has deteriorated and he will need to be admitted.'

'Oh, right. Maybe you could take a look at her, then, Dr
Constantine?'

Katie carefully kept all inflection out of her voice. She had
spent the night thinking about the decision she'd made to
clear her name. Although she knew it was what she needed to
do for her own peace of mind, it was the fact that it seemed
equally important to prove to Christos that she wasn't to blame
that bothered her. Why did she care what he thought about her?

'Of course.'

Katie forced the disquieting thought from her mind as she
led the way back to the temporary examination area. She had
a job to do and she refused to let anything get in the way of
her doing it to the best of her ability. 'This is Dr Constantine,'
she explained to the two women. 'Dr Constantine is in charge
of the trauma unit.'

'*Kalimera*.' Christos smiled at the women as he broke into
a stream of rapid Greek. Katie guessed that he was telling the
old lady that he needed to examine her so she went to the bed.
He nodded to her after he finished speaking. 'If you could
remove the sheet, please.'

Katie folded back the sheet that was covering the old lady's lower body and watched as he examined her. She couldn't help noticing how gentle he was as he explored the area around the old lady's right hip and groin.

'It looks as though the head of the femur has fractured. There appears to be considerable displacement, too. I'd like to send Mrs Mouskos for an X-ray, if you would arrange it, please, Nurse.'

'Of course,' Katie agreed, drawing the sheet over the old lady again.

'But the paramedics said that my aunt's hip was fractured,' the niece protested. 'Are you saying they were wrong?'

'Not at all.' Christos took a pen out of his pocket and picked up the patient's chart. 'What is commonly known as a fractured hip is actually a fracture of the neck of the femur— the thigh bone.'

He drew a sketch on the back of the notes and showed it to her. 'As you can see from this, the hip joint is like a ball and socket. The head of the femur is smooth and rounded, and it fits into a cup-like cavity in the pelvis called the acetabulum. From what I can tell, your aunt's femur has been fractured just below the socket.'

'I understand now.' The young woman frowned as she studied the diagram. 'Will the surgeons be able to mend it?'

'They will do their best, but it will take time to heal and your aunt might never regain full use of the leg,' he explained gently. 'Bones become thinner with age and it makes it that much more difficult to repair them.'

'But they will try?' the niece insisted. 'My aunt might be old but she is very active. I would like to think that she will regain her independence at some point.'

'The surgeons will do everything they can for her,' he assured her.

Katie turned away, not wanting him to see how surprised she was. She'd worked with a lot of consultants and few had taken the time to reassure a relative the way Christos had done.

It had been the same last night when she had met him at the harbour. He had done his best to reassure her then too. Had she been wrong to suspect him of having an ulterior motive?

She sighed. She had enough to think about without having to worry if she had been unfair to him. She had to concentrate on proving her innocence and forget about everything else. After all, she couldn't imagine that Christos would thank her if she proved that his cousin had been lying.

CHAPTER SIX

THE morning flew past. Fortunately, most of the holidaymakers who'd had food poisoning were well enough to be sent back to their hotel by the middle of the morning and that helped to relieve the pressure. By the time Katie went for her lunch, there was just a handful of people waiting to be seen. Maria invited her to have lunch in the canteen with her but she refused. It was a glorious day and it seemed a shame to waste it by sitting indoors, although the older nurse laughed when Katie told her that.

'Wait until it gets really hot,' Maria warned her. 'The temperature can reach more than 40 C in the summer. You will be very glad to stay indoors then.'

'I'm sure you're right.' Katie laughed. 'However, after the gloom of a Manchester spring, you can't imagine how wonderful it is to see the sun shining. I intend to make the most of it!'

She left Maria and made her way to the foyer. There was a café there so she bought herself a sandwich and a bottle of mineral water then went outside. Paths criss-crossed the grounds and she followed one of them until she came to a bench tucked between some flowering shrubs. There was a wonderful view over the bay from there so she sat down.

She had just finished her sandwich and put the wrapping into the bin when she heard footsteps coming along the path. The bench was tucked back amongst the bushes so she couldn't see who it was, but it sounded as though there were two people walking along the path. She frowned when she heard a man laugh. There was something familiar about the sound, although it was a moment before she realised it was Petros's voice she could hear.

A wave of panic rose inside her at the thought of seeing him again. Even though she'd made up her mind to confront him, she hadn't worked out what she intended to say to him yet. What if he denied telling her that he loved her, what would she do then? It would be her word against his and, as she knew to her cost, he would have little compunction about twisting the facts.

The thought of the scene that might ensue was too much to deal with. She scrambled to her feet and forced her way through the bushes just a moment before Petros came into view. There was a woman with him, although Katie could see very little of her apart from the fact that she had blonde hair. They reached the bench and stopped to admire the view, and her heart ached when she saw Petros drop a tender kiss on the woman's lips. Just a few weeks ago he had kissed her that way, too.

A wave of pain engulfed her as she hurried back inside the hospital. Even though Christos had told her that his cousin was marrying someone else, she hadn't fully believed it. Part of her had kept hoping that it would turn out to be some sort of terrible mistake. Now she was under no such illusions. Petros didn't want her. He never had. He'd just made use of her. And it was that last thought which was the hardest one of all to bear.

* * *

Christos had decided not to go to the staff canteen that day. He had a meeting with the finance committee after lunch and he wanted to go over the figures again. As head of trauma care, it was his job to ensure that sufficient funding was made available to them. There'd been quite a large cut proposed at the start of the month and although he had argued successfully against it, he couldn't afford to become complacent.

He bought himself a coffee and sat down at a table near the door. He'd brought the statistics sheets with him so he spread them out on the table. According to the figures, they were on course to meet all their targets. Patient numbers were up and waiting times were down. Recovery rates were also impressive. It seemed that the extra training he'd been doing with his team had paid off. If they could maintain these standards, the management would have no justification for implementing any cuts.

He was just gathering the sheets together when he heard footsteps hurrying across the foyer and he frowned when he saw Katie rush past. It was obvious that she was upset and he couldn't help wondering what had happened. Jamming the papers back into their folder, he hurried after her.

'Katie, wait!'

'I'm on my lunch-break.' She slowed down when she heard him calling her, although she didn't stop. 'I'm not due back at work for another ten minutes if you're checking up on me.'

'I'm not.' He put his hand on her arm and forced her to stop. 'What's wrong?'

'Nothing.'

'You know that isn't true. I can see that you're upset so tell me what's happened.'

'Why? What possible difference does it make to you? You

don't care about me, Christos. You only care about your precious cousin!'

She shrugged off his hand and hurried away. Christos didn't go after her, though, because there was no point. He sighed, wondering why it had stung so much to hear her say that. He had to put his cousin's interests first, yet he couldn't pretend that he was indifferent to Katie's feelings. It made him see what a difficult position he was in. Maybe he should get in touch with Petros and insist that he sorted this out. Once Katie had spoken to his cousin, surely she would realise her best option was to return to England.

The thought of her leaving should have reassured him, but it didn't. He realised with a sinking heart that he was going to miss her when she went. It might sound crazy, but he was becoming very attached to her and he would be sorry to see her leave, even though it would solve a lot of problems.

The afternoon got off to a slow start after the hectic pace of the morning but Katie was glad. She was still finding it difficult to come to terms with what she had witnessed in the garden that lunchtime. If she'd needed proof that Petros had never loved her, she had it now. She had been nothing more than a distraction for him while he'd been in England and it was painful to know just how little he had valued her.

She dealt with a couple of patients who had suffered fairly minor injuries—a man who had cut himself while using a saw and a woman who had dropped a heavy carton on her foot. Fortunately, the man's leg just needed cleaning and stitching; after a booster tetanus jab he was discharged.

The woman was in a lot of pain so Yanni asked Katie to arrange for her foot to be X-rayed. She took her to the radiography unit and waited until the films were ready. Two of the metatarsal bones were fractured so Yanni sent the patient off to the plaster room with a porter. They'd just left when Maria poked her head into the cubicle.

'Do either of you know where Christos has got to? I've tried his office but he isn't there.'

'He had a finance meeting after lunch,' Yanni explained. 'Why? What's happened?'

'We've just received a report that a speedboat has hit a ferry bringing tourists back from Coral Bay,' Maria explained worriedly. 'There's no information about the number of casualties yet, but it doesn't sound good.'

'I'll page Christos,' Yanni offered immediately.

Katie frowned as he hurried away. 'What do you want me to do?'

'Just carry on until Christos gets here. He'll want to organise us into teams if it's a major incident so it's best to wait until he arrives before we do anything.'

Maria hurried off to inform the rest of the staff about what had happened. Katie fetched her next patient, wondering which team she would be asked to work with. She sighed. One thing was certain—she couldn't see Christos asking her to work with him.

'I'm going to split us up into three teams. Yanni will head up team one, Melinda will be in charge of team two and I'll oversee team three.'

Christos glanced round to check that everyone was paying attention. In a situation like this every single person needed to know what his role would be or chaos would ensue. His gaze landed on Katie and he felt his heart lift when he saw the concentration on her face.

'Ariadne, Tina and Maria will be in team one. You'll be working in Resus with Yanni. Androu and Lara will be in team two with Melinda.' He turned to his junior registrar, Melinda Georgiou. 'I want you to concentrate on the less severely injured. We need to assess and treat them as quickly as possible because space will be at a premium. According to the latest report we've received, the ferry was carrying over two hundred people so it's going to get extremely busy in here in the next few hours.'

He carried on when Melinda nodded. 'Marina and Katie will be working with me as part of team three. We'll be travelling by helicopter to the section of the coast closest to where the accident happened and setting up a base there. Are you all clear what you should be doing?'

Once again he glanced around the room and this time he couldn't help noticing the surprise on Katie's face. It was obvious that she hadn't expected to be on his team and, if he was honest, he wasn't sure why he had chosen her. Being first on scene was the most demanding job. You never knew what you were going to encounter and had to be able to think on your feet. But for some reason his instinct had been to take Katie.

The meeting broke up and everyone went to get ready. Christos led the way to the storeroom. 'Flight suits and everything else you need is in here,' he explained, switching on the lights.

Katie glanced round as she followed him into the room. 'We just help ourselves?'

'Yes.' He pointed to a row of pegs which held the bright orange flight suits. 'Smallest sizes start at that end.'

'Thanks.'

She headed to the end of the row and unhooked a suit. Kicking off her shoes, she slipped it on without any more ado. Christos unhooked a larger suit for himself, silently chalking it up as a point in her favour. A lot of people would have made a fuss about being asked to take part in this exercise but she was merely getting on with job. It made him wonder once again how much of what Petros had told him had been true. He certainly hadn't seen any sign of the demanding, neurotic woman his cousin had described at such length.

The thought was deeply disquieting but he knew that he couldn't dwell on it right then. As soon as they were ready, they headed up to the roof where the helicopter was waiting for them. Katie scrambled on board and took her seat. She fastened her safety harness and attached the radio mike to her helmet then helped Marina with hers. Christos's brows rose as he watched her.

'Have you done this before?'

'Yes. I did a stint with HEMS—the helicopter emergency medical services. A lot of the incidents we were called to attend were RTAs, though, so this will be something completely new for me. I've never been to an incident at sea before.'

'It's not something I have a lot of experience of either,' he admitted. 'Fortunately, this type of accident is pretty rare.'

'What kind of injuries do you think we'll encounter?'

'Fractures, shock, possibly some burns injuries, although, from what I can gather, only the speedboat caught fire.' He switched on his microphone as the helicopter's engines roared to life. 'My advice is to be prepared for anything and that way you won't be too surprised by what you find.'

'I'll bear it in mind,' she agreed, smiling at him from behind her own mouthpiece.

Christos turned and stared out of the window as the helicopter lifted off. The ground was rushing past below at dizzying speed, although maybe it was his head that was whirling and making him feel so giddy. The more he learned about Katie, the more he liked about her, and it was confusing to feel this way. Although he had been out with several women since he had split up with Eleni, he had never felt as drawn to any of them as he was to Katie. There was just something about her that appealed to him on a deeper level.

He sighed when he realised how fruitless it was to harbour such thoughts. Even without the complication of her relationship with Petros, there was his own track record to consider. His work was still vitally important to him and he couldn't imagine that ever changing. He simply didn't have the time to spare to build a lasting relationship with anyone.

'His temperature's just above 34 C. He's hypothermic so we need to warm him up and make sure it doesn't drop any lower.'

Katie could see the concern on Christos's face as he bent over the child. Four-year-old Dylan Walters had been on the speedboat with his parents when the accident had happened. Fortunately, the family had managed to jump overboard before the boat had caught fire, but they had been in the water for some time before they had been rescued. Dylan's temperature had dropped to worrying levels during his immersion and it was vital that they stop it falling any further.

Taking a pair of scissors out of her pack, she sliced through the little boy's clothing then rubbed him dry. His skin was the colour of putty and he appeared too listless to cry as she

wrapped him in a space blanket, pulling the end over his head
to stop him losing any more body heat. Christos was checking
the child's pulse again and he frowned.

'I'm going to have him ferried back to hospital by helicopter. His pulse is far too slow and his respiration rate is down,
too. It's difficult to raise the body temperature when it reaches
this point, especially with a young child. He'll need controlled warming, so the sooner he's in ICU the better.'

'Shall I tell the parents?' she offered.

'Please. The coastguard has just brought some more people
ashore and I need to check on them.'

'No problem.'

Katie got up and went over to where the little boy's parents
were sitting. They had set up a triage area on the beach. As
soon as the passengers from the ferry were brought ashore,
they were assessed according to the severity of their injuries.
Walking wounded were being taken straight to hospital by
mini-bus—their injuries would be dealt with there. The more
seriously injured were stabilised first and transported by ambulance. The very worst cases were being flown back by helicopter as soon as they were able to be moved. Dylan's
parents had been classed as walking wounded: the child's
mother had a cut on her forehead and his father had injured
his hand. They both leapt up when Katie appeared.

'How is he?' Amy Walters demanded.

'He's suffering from hypothermia, I'm afraid.'

'But that can't be right,' Mrs Walters protested. 'It's a beautiful day and the sun is shining, so how can he be suffering
from the cold?'

'The sun may be shining but the temperature in the sea is
several degrees lower than it is on land,' Katie explained pa-

tiently. 'Dylan was in the water for quite a long time and that's why he's so cold. The doctor thinks that he will need controlled warming, which will have to be done in the intensive care unit at the hospital.'

'Controlled warming…you mean you'll warm him up with hot-water bottles?' Dylan's father put in.

'It's a bit more complicated than that,' she told him gently. 'Dylan will be attached to a machine that will withdraw his blood, warm it and return it to his body. It's the most effective way of dealing with severe cases of hypothermia.'

'Oh!' Amy put her hand over her mouth. 'My poor baby! I knew we shouldn't have gone out in that stupid boat. I told you so, Fred, didn't I?'

'There's no point arguing about it now,' Katie hurriedly intervened as the woman rounded on her husband. 'Dylan needs to be moved to hospital immediately. There isn't room in the helicopter for you, I'm afraid, so you will have to follow on in one of the mini-buses.'

'But I want to go with him,' Amy protested, clutching hold of Katie's arm.

'I'm sorry but it isn't possible to take you,' she said firmly, removing the woman's hand. 'We need every bit of available space for the injured.'

'Then I'm not going to let you take Dylan,' Amy stated belligerently. 'He's my son and he isn't going anywhere without me.'

'If Dylan doesn't have this treatment, he could die.' Katie looked at the young woman, wondering if it was shock that was causing her to behave so unreasonably. While she sympathised with her, her main concern was the child's welfare. 'Are you prepared to take that risk, Mrs Walters?'

'No, of course she isn't,' Fred said, butting in. He shook his head when his wife started to protest. 'Just shut up, Amy, and let them do their job. It may be my fault for taking you on that boat trip but I won't be responsible for risking my son's life just so you can have your own way.'

Katie left them to argue it out and went back to the little boy. Marina was getting him ready for the transfer; she rolled her eyes when Katie knelt beside her. 'That doesn't look like a marriage that was made in heaven.'

'It certainly doesn't,' Katie agreed as she fastened the last couple of straps on the stretcher. 'There seems to be a lot of friction going on there.'

'It's a real minefield, isn't it?' Marina grimaced. 'I mean, you fall in love and think you're going to live happily ever after, like in all the fairy stories. The trouble is that most people don't take the time to get to know each other. It's no wonder so many couples split up once they realise the person they thought was their soul mate is actually a complete stranger.'

Marina went to check on another patient who was being prepared for transfer. Katie double-checked that Dylan was securely strapped into the stretcher then helped the crew load him on board the helicopter. The boy's parents watched what was happening in complete silence. Relations between them were obviously strained and she couldn't help thinking about what Marina had said. Had they, too, fallen in love and assumed it would be enough to guarantee a lifetime of happiness?

It was what so many people did, her own parents included. They had married then spent the rest of their lives regretting it. She had tried to avoid making the same mistake, but even though she hadn't rushed into an affair with Petros, it still hadn't worked out.

The truth was that nobody could be certain that a relationship would last. Maybe Kelly was right to turn her back on love. Maybe she should do the same and never put herself in that position again. Love simply wasn't worth the heartache.

Her gaze went to Christos, who was helping to carry a stretcher up the beach, and she frowned. She couldn't imagine Christos letting a woman down. Once he had made a commitment, he would stick to it. He wouldn't lie or cheat to get a woman into his bed either. He wouldn't need to. The woman Christos chose as his lover would be the luckiest woman in the world.

Her face burned as she turned away before he caught her staring at him. She had no idea where that thought had sprung from but there was no chance of her testing out that theory. She and Christos certainly weren't destined to become lovers.

CHAPTER SEVEN

BY THE time evening started to draw in they had dealt with over a hundred casualties. Thankfully, the majority of the people they'd seen had suffered only minor injuries—cuts, bruises, shock. Of the more severely injured, just three had given real cause for concern and they had been transferred to hospital. As they started to clear up, Christos realised that they had been extremely fortunate that day.

'It wasn't nearly as bad as I feared it would be.'

He sighed when Katie unwittingly echoed that same sentiment. It was amazing how in tune they seemed to be. As he had soon discovered, she seemed able to second-guess his every request. It wasn't just the rapport they had established so quickly that had impressed him either. She had handled the job with grace and good humour. It had been extremely stressful, dealing with so many terrified people, but not once had she shown a hint of impatience. He was more convinced than ever that Petros had been spinning him a line.

'We got off quite lightly,' he agreed, realising that it was becoming increasingly important to him to clear Katie's name. He had accepted what his cousin had told him, but now he could see how unfair it had been of him to do that. It was a relief when Marina came over to ask him if she could accept a lift back to the hospital because it made him feel so guilty to wonder if he had misjudged Katie.

'Of course. We've just about finished here so you get off. Thank you for all your hard work today, Marina. You did a first-rate job. You, too, Katie, of course,' he added hastily, in case she thought he was leaving her out.

'Don't mention it.' Katie avoided his eyes as she picked up her backpack. 'I'll see if I can hitch a lift back with Marina.'

She turned to leave but not before Christos had seen the hurt in her eyes. 'I meant what I said,' he said firmly. 'You're a highly skilled nurse and I'm really glad you were on my team today.'

'But you'd still prefer it if I wasn't here?' Her eyes lifted to his and he could see the challenge they held. 'That is how you feel, isn't it?'

'Yes.' He could hear the edge in his voice but he hated being put on the spot, especially when he was feeling so ambivalent. 'I still believe you should leave the island and forget about Petros.'

'And that's exactly what I intend to do—after I've seen him.' Her face was set as she swung the bag over her shoulder. 'I know you think that I am the guilty party, Christos, but the only thing I'm guilty of is being stupid enough to be taken in by your cousin's lies. I intend to make him admit what he's done and apologise for it.'

'Even if it means another woman getting hurt?' he said through gritted teeth. The pain in her voice was almost more than he could stand. He wanted to take her in his arms and comfort her but he knew it wasn't what she would want. She wasn't interested in him; she only cared about his cousin. It was oddly painful to have to face that fact.

'No. Eleni doesn't need to be involved, although I do wonder if it's in her best interests to be kept in the dark. If Petros can do this to me then he could do the same thing to her, too.'

'The situation is completely different. Petros is in love with Eleni and he would never be unfaithful to *her*,' he said harshly, because the thought had stung. Why did he suddenly wish with all his heart that it was him whom Katie loved? It didn't make sense.

'Let's hope you're right,' she said in a tight little voice.

Too late he realised how much it must have hurt her to hear him say that. He realised that he needed to keep his emotions under control. After all, he was just a bystander in this situation, the voice of reason. Although he was no longer in love with Eleni, he did care about her and wanted her to be happy. And making sure that nothing ruined her wedding day was the best way he could do that.

'I'm sorry. That wasn't very tactful of me. I know what Petros can be like, but he's different with Eleni. He really does love her.'

'As he never really loved me?' She laughed harshly. 'I understand. It's partly my own fault. I shouldn't have been so gullible. I should have realised he had an ulterior motive for telling me he loved me!'

Christos winced when he heard how bitter she sounded. His cousin had a lot to answer for, he thought grimly. 'How long did you and Petros go out together?' He shrugged when she looked at him in surprise. 'You don't have to tell me if you don't want to.'

'It's not that. It's the fact that you seem to have accepted that we did have a relationship that surprises me. Have you decided that I might have been telling you the truth after all?'

'I don't think the situation is as straightforward as my cousin claimed,' he said carefully, because he didn't want to make the mistake of allowing his emotions to surface again. There was no point admitting that he had doubts about what Petros had said until he had spoken to him. After that, he could decide for himself who had been telling the truth.

She smiled wryly. 'Still hedging your bets, Christos?'

'Not at all. My main aim is still the same. I still intend to ensure that nothing happens to disrupt this wedding.'

'Of course. Silly of me to imagine that you might be having second thoughts about me.'

He sighed. 'I was wrong to speak to you the way I did when you arrived, and I apologise for it. I can see now that Petros has been somewhat economical with the truth.'

'Thank you. It's not nice to be thought of as someone who would deliberately set out to ruin another person's life.'

He heard the catch in her voice and felt worse than ever when he recalled all the things he'd said to her. 'I don't think you would do that, Katie. However, you could still cause a lot of heartache. Won't you reconsider and accept that your relationship with Petros is over?'

'I wish I could, but I shall never be able to move on until he admits what he's done. All I can do is promise you that I will be careful. I don't want to hurt Eleni, that's why I didn't say anything to him at lunchtime.'

'What do you mean? Are you saying that you saw Petros today?'

'Yes. He was at the hospital with Eleni. Oh, don't worry, they didn't see me. I made sure of that. I need to work out exactly what I intend to say to him first. I want him to understand what he did to me, and stop him doing it to anyone else.'

'There isn't going to be anyone else after he marries Eleni,' Christos said sharply, hoping he wasn't tempting fate.

'Let's hope you're right.' She gave him a sad little smile and turned away.

Christos's hands clenched. She looked so forlorn that once again he longed to comfort her, but he knew how impossible it would be. Katie didn't want him—she wanted his cousin.

Pain swept through him again but he forced it down. He piled the rest of their equipment together so it could be taken back to the hospital. The helicopter had returned to base so he would have to travel back in one of the ambulances. He was about to start shifting everything up to the road when a police officer came hurrying over to him.

'We've received a message about a missing person,' the officer explained. 'A Dutch man by the name of Eric Van der Halk boarded the ferry this morning and he hasn't returned.'

Christos's heart sank. 'Have you checked the list of casualties who've been taken to the hospital?'

'*Ne.*' The officer nodded. 'His name isn't on it and he hasn't returned to his hotel. His wife reported him missing so we are going to do another search of the shore.'

'I'll stay and help.' Christos put the supplies back on the ground. 'If he is here then he's probably been injured and it will save time if I'm here to treat him.' He glanced round when he heard footsteps hurrying over the shingle and frowned when he saw Katie coming towards them. 'I thought you'd gone back with Marina?'

'I was just about to leave when I heard about the missing man,' she explained. 'I thought you might need some help.'

'Are you sure you want to stay? It's way past the time you should have finished your shift.'

'It doesn't matter. Anyway, I want to help—if you'll let me, of course.'

He heard the uncertainty in her voice and hurried to reassure her. Even though he had apologised for the way he had behaved, she was still very wary of him and he couldn't blame her. 'I'd be very glad of your help,' he said truthfully, and was rewarded by a smile.

'That's OK, then.'

She knelt down and started to sort through their supplies, setting aside any items she thought they would need. Christos watched her for a second then turned away. It was just a smile, he told himself sternly as he followed the officer to where the search party was assembling. Nevertheless, it felt as though a weight had been lifted off his shoulders all of a sudden. Although they may not agree about her intention to stay on the island, at least it appeared they could be friends, and that was something to be grateful for.

He sighed under his breath. Friendship was all very well but if he was honest with himself, he knew that he wanted more than that from her.

Katie hurriedly put together a fresh pack of supplies. She knew that the search would need to get under way as soon as possible. If the missing man had been washed up along the coast then it was vital that they find him before night fell. She had just finished getting everything ready when Christos came back.

'We're going to do a search of the bay. According to the coastguard, if he fell overboard, the prevailing currents would have washed him ashore somewhere around here.'

'I wonder why nobody spotted him before,' she said,

snapping the locks on the haversack. She started to heft it onto her shoulder but Christos took it from her.

'I'll carry this, you take the torch.' He swung the bag over his shoulder and handed her the torch. 'I'm not sure why he wasn't found before but, apparently, there's a network of caves along this stretch of the coast. It's possible that he's been washed into one of them so we're going to check them out.'

Katie grimaced. 'Isn't the tide coming in?'

'Yes, which makes it imperative that we find him soon.'

Katie didn't say anything as she followed him across the shingle. She knew how urgent the situation was. The missing tourist could drown if he was trapped in one of the caves when the tide came in. They joined the rest of the search party and waited while a list of names was made. Whistles were handed out and torches distributed to those who didn't have one. The daylight was fading fast and every precaution had to be taken to ensure their own safety.

Once they were properly equipped, they were assigned to a group. Their group consisted of her and Christos, a police officer and a couple of local fishermen who knew that section of the coast. They were to search the west side of the bay. A second team would search the east side and the third team would scour the central area.

'Stick close to me,' Christos instructed as they set off. 'If you find that you're lagging behind, shout out. I don't want you getting lost out here in the dark.'

'Neither do I.' Katie shivered as she stared across the rocky terrain. Now that the sun had almost disappeared, the coast-line looked very inhospitable. 'Do you think we'll find him?'

'Let's hope so.'

Christos's tone was grim. It was obvious that he didn't rate the man's chances if they failed to find him. Katie followed him to the foreshore where they fanned out into a line so they could cover a larger area. The ground was treacherous underfoot and there was a constant danger of them tripping over on the rocks. It was slow going and they'd barely covered half a mile when the sun began to dip below the horizon. One of the fishermen suddenly stopped and pointed towards an outcrop of rocks. Katie turned to Christos.

'I don't understand what he's saying.'

'Apparently, there's a cave just beyond those rocks. He thinks we should check it out before we go any further.'

'Right.' She hurried forward then gasped when her foot suddenly slid into a crevice, causing her to stumble.

'Careful!' Christos grabbed her arm and hauled her upright.

'Thanks.' Katie gingerly eased her foot from between the rocks. 'Good job you were here or I'd have gone flat on my face.'

'And probably broken your ankle. Make sure it's all right before you try walking on it. You might have sprained it.'

'I don't think so.' She leant against him for support as she tested her weight on the foot. 'No, it's fine. Just a bit of a twinge but nothing serious.'

'Are you sure?'

Katie frowned when she heard the uneven tenor of his voice. She looked up in surprise and felt her breath catch when she saw the strain on his face. All of a sudden she became aware of the intimacy of their position. She was using his body as a prop, her back resting against his chest, her bottom nestling between his thighs. She had taken off her flight suit when she'd arrived and all she had on now was the uniform top and pants she wore in the hospital. The fabric was so thin that she could feel the heat of his body flowing through it, feel the solid strength of the muscles in his chest and thighs pressing against her. She bit her lip because she couldn't remember ever being so aware of a man's body before.

'Quite sure.'

She straightened abruptly, switching on the torch as she picked her way across the rocks. She wasn't sure what was going on, but there was no point denying that she had responded to Christos's nearness. That had been a big enough shock, but what made it so much worse was that he had responded to her too. She had felt his body quicken as he'd held her and it was pointless pretending it hadn't happened. For a few brief seconds he had forgotten about the threat she posed to his cousin and had responded to her as a man responded to a woman he desired.

CHAPTER EIGHT

WHAT in heaven's name was going on?

As Christos made his way across the rocks to where the rest of the search party had gathered, he found it hard to believe what had happened. One minute he'd been trying to stop Katie having a nasty fall and the next he'd been thinking the kind of thoughts he hadn't harboured about a woman for years. He knew that Katie wasn't interested in him. It was his cousin she wanted. However, when he had held her in his arms just now, his body had made its needs perfectly clear.

Christos bit back a groan of dismay. The thought that Katie might have noticed how aroused he'd been filled him with embarrassment. It was hard to hide how wretched he felt as he joined the others. Nikos—the fisherman who had pointed out the cave—was peering over the edge of the rocks. When Christos approached, he could see that there was quite a steep drop below. By lying flat on his stomach, he could just make out the entrance to the cave. The tide was coming in fast now and already the first waves were lapping against the shore.

'Do you think the missing tourist has been washed up in there?'

He glanced round when Katie spoke to him, steeling himself not to betray any hint of emotion. 'I've no idea. Someone will have to climb down there and check.'

He'd barely finished speaking when the police officer swung himself over the ledge. He disappeared into the cave only to reappear a moment later, waving frantically.

'Looks as though we've found him,' Christos observed as he stood up. 'I'll go down and take a look at him.'

'Shall I come with you?' she offered immediately but he shook his head.

'Let me check how he is first. It might not be necessary for you to make the climb down there as well.'

'You think he's dead?'

'I don't know until I've examined him,' he said sharply. He sighed when he saw her face close up because it wasn't fair to take his frustration out on her. 'Sorry. I didn't mean to snap at you. Let's not give up hope just yet.'

He swung himself over the ledge and scrambled down the rocks to where the policeman was waiting. 'How is he? Is he alive?'

'I couldn't tell. It's so dark in there and with the noise of the waves and everything…' The officer broke off and shrugged.

'Right. I'll check him over. Whatever happens, though, we're going to need some more light down here. Can you get everyone to pass their torches down to us, please?'

The officer relayed his request while Christos made his way inside the cave. The entrance was quite low and he had to bend double, but once he was inside, he was able to straighten up. The missing man was at the very back of the cave, lying face-down on the ground. Christos could see there was a large wound on the back of his head so his hopes weren't high when he knelt beside him. Placing his fingers on the carotid artery, he checked the man's pulse and was surprised when he detected a faint rhythm.

'He's alive,' he shouted to the policeman, who was standing just inside the entrance. 'I'm going to need a stretcher down here and an ambulance on standby.'

'*Ne.*'

The officer hurried away while Christos bent over the casualty again. He checked the man's skull first to assess the extent of the damage. The scalp had been split open and had bled profusely. Dried blood encrusted the back of the man's head, making it difficult to see the wound clearly, but there was a definite indentation in the skull which indicated a severe head trauma. His main concern now was to stabilise the patient in readiness for immediate transfer to hospital

'I've got the extra torches you need. How is he?'

Christos glanced round when Katie appeared. 'Severe head trauma. His skull is definitely fractured, although I've no way of assessing how much damage has been done.'

'He'll need a CT scan when we get him to hospital.'

She switched on the torches and arranged them in a semi-circle so that they lit up the area where they were working. Once again, Christos was struck by her professionalism. It didn't seem to matter that they were in a cave with the tide coming in because she was completely focussed on their patient's needs. How could a woman like this be guilty of all the things his cousin had accused her of doing?

In that moment he realised that he had to make Petros tell him the truth as soon as possible. Up till now his main concern had been to protect Eleni by making sure the wedding plans weren't ruined, but that wasn't enough any more. He was becoming increasingly concerned about Katie; her happiness mattered to him more than anything else.

The thought stunned him. A week ago he had never imagined that he would feel this way about a woman ever again. What had happened all those years ago between him and Eleni had made him wary of falling in love. If he hadn't been able to make their relationship work then what chance did he have of finding love and making a lasting commitment to another woman? But all of a sudden he felt differently. He was no longer content to let life pass him by, to sit on sidelines with only his career for company. He wanted more from life than a job. Much more. He wanted a proper home and someone to share it with, some one he could love.

He glanced at Katie and felt his heart fill with longing. It had been Katie's advent into his life which had made him reassess his priorities. She had shown him what he was missing. It might sound crazy to say so but he knew that if he had Katie in his life then he would want for nothing more.

'Do you want me to set up a drip now, or should I wait until we've got him out of here?'

Katie looked up after she finished putting a dressing over the back of the patient's head. Christos didn't appear to have heard her question so she repeated it, and saw him jump. It was obvious that he had been deep in thought and she had an uncomfortable feeling that she knew what he'd been thinking about, too.

'You can set it up now. He's very dehydrated and I'd like to get some fluids into him as quickly as possible.'

'Fine.' Opening the backpack, she took out a bag of saline, trying not to think about what might have been troubling him, but it was impossible. Her cheeks burned as she recalled the urgent pressure of his body when he'd held her earlier. She wasn't naïve and understood that a man could desire a woman even if he wasn't in love with her. However, it was the fact that Christos had wanted *her* that surprised her. How could he feel that way if he believed his cousin's claims?

The thought that he might be changing his mind about her made her heart lift. Before she left Cyprus, she wanted to be sure that Christos knew the truth about what had gone on between her and Petros. She couldn't bear to think that he would always have doubts about her.

'Here—you can hang the bag on this,' he instructed, wedging a piece of driftwood into a crevice in the rock.

'Thanks.' Katie smiled as she hooked the bag of saline over the wood. 'You must have a been a Scout when you were younger—always prepared.'

'I wish.' He laughed. 'I'm afraid. I couldn't get the hang of starting a camp fire by rubbing a couple of sticks together.'

'Me neither. I was hopeless when we went camping, although Kelly was brilliant at it.'

'It was lucky you had her to help you.'

'Oh, it was. How about you? Do you have any brothers or sisters who came to your aid?'

'No. I'm an only child so I had to muddle through as best I could.'

'That's a shame.' She grinned at him. 'I was always so glad that I had a sister the same age as me. We got each other out of all sorts of scrapes.'

'It sounds as though you two are really close,' he observed, checking the patient's pulse.

'We are. Obviously, it makes a difference when you're a

twin. There's already a special bond between you. But we've grown even closer since our parents died.'

'When did they die? Was it very recent?'

'Yes.' She sighed. 'Mum had a heart attack two years ago. She'd always been extremely healthy so it was a huge shock for everyone, and especially for my father.' She frowned. 'It was really strange how hard it hit him, in fact.'

'Why do say that?' he asked, glancing up.

'My parents got divorced when Kelly and I were ten. They had spent years arguing and the arguments continued even after they'd split up. Neither remarried and I always assumed it was because they didn't want to risk making another mistake. Yet when Mum died, Dad went to pieces. He had a stroke at the start of this year and he just gave up.' She shrugged. 'I don't think he could face the thought of carrying on living without Mum, even though they'd made each other's lives hell for years.'

'It's sometimes difficult to make a relationship work, even though you love one another,' he said quietly. 'I'm sure your parents loved each other despite the fact that they found it impossible to live together.'

'Do you think so?' Katie said, wondering why that thought had never occurred to her. She had focussed exclusively on the negative side of her parents' marriage, but there had been good times, too, times when they'd had fun together as a family. She just hadn't remembered them.

It was a shock to realise that her view of her childhood had been distorted. It was en effort to concentrate when Christos continued speaking.

'It must have been tremendously stressful for you. Losing both your parents in such a short space of time must have been very difficult.'

'It was.' Extremely difficult, she thought. It wasn't long after her father had died that she'd agreed to go out with Petros, in fact. Had grief helped to drive her into his arms? Petros had been so attentive and she had needed comfort so much, but would she have got involved with him if she'd been less vulnerable?

She had never considered that possibility before, and it made her feel very uneasy to wonder if her feelings for Petros had been influenced by outside circumstances. She hurried on, not wanting Christos to know that she was having such doubts. 'What about your parents? Do they live in Cyprus?'

'No. They died in an accident when I was thirteen years old. They were keen sailors and spent every weekend in the summer on their boat. They were coming back from a trip around the island when they were caught in a freak storm and their boat capsized.'

'How awful!' she exclaimed. 'Were you with them at the time?'

'No. I used to get bored if I was on the boat for too long so my parents had left me with my aunt and uncle that day—Petros's parents.' He shrugged. 'The court appointed them as my legal guardians and I lived with them until I went to university.'

'At least you had someone you knew to take care of you,' she said quietly, thinking that it explained an awful lot. He'd been brought up with his cousin so he was bound to feel an allegiance to him. It made her see how hard it would be to convince him that Petros had been lying about her. Christos's loyalties were bound to lie with his cousin.

The thought was so depressing that she found it difficult to hide her dismay. Fortunately, Christos was checking their patient's obs and he didn't appear to notice that anything was wrong. He looked up and she could see the concern in his eyes.

'His pulse has speeded up. Check his blood pressure again, will you?'

Katie hurriedly checked the reading on the digital sphygmomanometer. 'It's dropping.'

'Damn! There must be internal bleeding, either inside his skull or more likely elsewhere in his body. I need to examine him but I don't want to put any undue pressure on the back of his skull. The parietal bones could be fragmented and we can't risk any further displacement.'

'I can support his head,' she suggested, understanding the urgency of the situation. If the patient's BP dropped too low, vital organs would be starved of oxygen, causing irreversible damage.

'Yes, but we will have to extremely careful how we move him. We don't know if there's any spinal damage.'

'Do you want me to try and put a collar on him?'

'No. It's too difficult to fit one from this position. We'll wait until we've turned him over.'

Katie nodded. She moved a couple of the torches out of the way then knelt down so that she was behind the injured man. From this position she would be able to support his head and neck as they rolled him over.

'Nice and steady now,' Christos instructed as he straightened the man's legs to make it easier to turn him over. He looked round when the policeman came hurrying into the cave.

Katie waited in silence while the man relayed a message to Christos. 'What's happened?' she demanded, as soon as the officer had finished speaking.

'The tide is coming in fast,' Christos told her grimly. 'The fishermen think it will be no more than ten minutes before the water reaches the cave.'

'Ten minutes?' she gasped. 'But we need more time than that!'

'We'll just have to do the best we can.'

Katie didn't waste time arguing. The man's breathing was becoming increasingly laboured and she know that it was imperative they turn him over. Christos told the policeman to take hold of the man's legs while he supported his hips.

'On my count,' he instructed. 'One, two, three.'

They rolled the man onto his back with the minimum of fuss. Katie carefully supported the man's head while Christos examined him. She had placed a dressing over the wound on the back of his head to minimise the risk of infection but she wanted to make sure no pressure was put on the damaged section of skull. Christos frowned as he examined the patient's chest.

'I think it could be a haemothorax.'

'Is there any sign of injury to the chest wall?'

'No, but several ribs appear to have been broken. If a broken rib has pierced the surrounding tissue then blood could have been collecting in the pleural cavity. It's probably reached the point where it's compressed the lung and caused a partial collapse.' He opened the pack of medical supplies they'd brought with them and took out a plastic bottle and a length of plastic tubing. 'I'm going to have to drain the pleural cavity so the lung can reinflate.'

'Of course….' Katie broke off and gasped. 'Look! There's sea water coming into the cave!'

Christos turned towards the entrance. Although it was only a trickle as yet, he knew it wouldn't be long before the cave started to fill up. He came to a swift decision. 'I want you out of here right now.'

'No.' She shook her head. 'You can't manage this on your own, Christos. You need me to help you so I'm staying.'

He could tell that it was pointless arguing with her, especially when they both knew that she was right. Although he hated the thought of putting her at risk this way, he had no choice in the matter.

'All right, you can stay for now. But if I tell you to leave again, I don't want any arguments. Is that clear?'

'Yes.' She showed the policeman how to support the injured man's head then came round to help Christos, quickly cutting through the patient's clothing. 'You'll need to insert the tube just about here in his right side?' she clarified.

'Yes, that's fine.'

He put on some gloves while she swabbed the site where he would make the incision. Taking a scalpel out of the sterile pack of instruments, he sliced through the flesh then cut through the tough intercostal muscle, widening the incision he'd made with his fingertip until it was big enough to insert the tube. Blood immediately began to escape from the pleural space and collect in the bottle.

'His breathing is easing,' Katie announced. She checked the man's pulse. 'His pulse is stronger, too.'

'Good. Let's get that stretcher in here and move him out.'

Katie resumed her place by the patient's head while the officer went away to fetch the stretcher. More water was flowing into the cave, trickling across the sand towards where they were sitting. Christos picked up a torch and shone it around the walls to see how high the water level might rise. There was a tide mark three-quarters of the way up the walls, which he estimated to be at a height of roughly two metres. Although the water shouldn't completely fill the cave, it would be deep enough to be dangerous.

'It's time you left,' he said firmly, turning to Katie.

'Let me stay until the stretcher arrives,' she pleaded. 'I promise you that I'll go then, but I don't want to leave you here on your own in case something goes wrong.'

'All right,' he agreed, albeit reluctantly. He got up and went to the entrance of the cave, ducking down so he could see out. From that position all he could see was the black expanse of the sea lapping against the rocks. He jumped back as a huge wave swept ashore and came spilling into the cave. At this rate, the place would be flooded before the stretcher arrived.

The next few minutes were extremely tense. Although they did their best to protect the injured man, the cave was rapidly filling up with water. Christos had reached the point where he was wondering if help would arrive in time when the paramedics appeared. They'd brought a spinal board with them so they slid it under the man then moved him onto an inflatable stretcher, using padded supports to protect his head.

'It's not going to be easy to get this out of the cave with the tide coming in,' Christos warned them. 'I want one of you to go outside and get ready to grab hold of the stretcher as soon as we push it out. Katie, you're to leave first and make your way back to the rest of the group.'

This time she didn't object. She quickly waded through the water to the entrance. She was just about to duck under the rock when another wave rushed in and completely bowled her off her feet.

'Are you all right?' Christos shouted in alarm as he hurried towards her. He helped her to her feet, his eyes grazing over her body to check for any sign of injury.

'I'm fine.' She gave him a quick smile and his heart lifted when he saw the warmth in her eyes. 'The only thing injured is my pride. I didn't plan on getting such a soaking!'

Christos laughed softly, admiring the fact that she could make fun of herself at such a time. He helped her to the opening and waited while she ducked under the rim of the cave. He didn't have time to help her up the rocks as he would have liked to do, though. The water was up to his knees now and they would have to move quickly if they didn't want to be trapped inside the cave. While they could probably swim out of there, the injured man couldn't, and there was no way that he was prepared to leave him there.

It took a lot of manoeuvring but eventually they got the stretcher out of the cave. Willing hands were waiting to help them, but even so it wasn't easy to get it to safety. It was a relief when they got back to the ambulance, especially when Christos spotted Katie sitting on the rear steps with a blanket wrapped around her. He hadn't realised until that moment just how worried he'd been about her, but at least she was safe and that was the main thing.

She jumped up when she saw them approaching and came rushing over. 'How is he?'

'Still breathing, so that's something to be grateful for.' He groaned as he relinquished his end of the stretcher and flexed his aching muscles. 'Remind me not to try that again in a hurry, will you?'

She laughed. 'Not the easiest rescue, was it?'

'It certainly wasn't.' He smiled back, feeling his heart suffuse with warmth when he saw the understanding in her eyes. It felt so good to be able to share this moment with her. 'I think I'll stick to hospital work from now on,' he joked. 'It's far less strenuous.'

'I can't imagine you settling for the easy option,' she scoffed. 'It just isn't you.'

'No?' He cocked a brow. 'So what is "me"?' he asked, drawing imaginary quotation marks around the word.

'Hmm, I think you're someone who puts his job before everything else, including your personal comfort.'

'That could apply to you too,' he said, feeling a buzz of heat run along his veins at her very accurate assessment of him. He did put all his energy into doing his job. He always had. Some people would see that as a fault but it hadn't sounded as though Katie had been criticising him. Just the opposite. Heat poured through him because it he wasn't mistaken, she had meant it as a compliment.

'I suppose so. I know that my job is very important to me.'

'Then it seems we have something in common.'

One of the paramedics asked him a question just then so the subject was dropped. However, the thought stayed with him on the journey back to the hospital. He had never expected to feel so in tune with Katie, yet the more time he spent with her, the more he found himself drawn to her. Did she feel the same way? She may admire his dedication to his work, but it was what she thought of him as a person that seemed far more important at that moment. Did she actually like him?

It shouldn't have made a scrap of difference what she thought, of course, but there was no use pretending. He wanted her to like him. He wanted it very much indeed.

CHAPTER NINE

KATIE was glad when the ambulance dropped her off outside the hospital. Traveling back in her wet clothes hadn't made for the most comfortable of journeys. Fortunately, their patient seemed to be holding his own so that was some consolation. She left Christos to supervise the unloading and headed into the department, smiling when she saw Maria's surprise as she walked through the door.

'Katie! What's happened?' the older nurse exclaimed in dismay. 'You're soaking wet.'

'I took an unscheduled dip in the sea.' She glanced down at her wet clothes and grimaced. 'I couldn't borrow a spare set of scrubs to go home in, could I? The driver might not let me get on the bus looking like this.'

'Of course you can.' Maria hurried around the desk then stopped dead when Christos appeared. She shook her head when she saw the state of him. 'Not you as well. What on earth have you two been up to?'

'We got stuck in a cave with the tide coming in,' he explained succinctly. He turned to Katie and her heart seemed to leap into her throat when she saw the concern in his eyes.

'You should get changed. You'll catch a chill if you don't find something dry to wear.'

'That's just what we were about to do when you arrived,' Maria said firmly, immediately taking charge. She ushered Katie into the theatre suite and opened the door to the women's changing room. 'There's clean scrubs on the shelf. Just help yourself.'

'Thanks.' Katie smiled gratefully as she took a clean set of clothes off the shelf. 'How did you get on in here? It must have been really busy.'

'Oh, it was fine,' Maria said airily. 'What about you? How did *you* get on?'

'It was a bit hectic at times but we coped,' Katie replied, helping herself to a towel as well.

'I didn't mean that.' Maria smiled. 'I'm more interested in how you and Christos got on—*together*.'

Katie felt a wash of heat run up her face when she realised what Maria meant. 'Christos was in charge and I carried out his instructions,' she said carefully. 'What more can I say?'

'A lot.' Maria grinned at her. 'I've known Christos for a long time and I've never seen him look so concerned about a member of staff before. It's obvious that there's something going on between you two.'

'There's nothing going on between me and Christos,' Katie denied hurriedly. Although she liked Maria, she certainly didn't want to be drawn into a discussion about her relationship with Christos.

Her heart lurched at the thought of her and Christos having a relationship and she rushed on. 'Honestly.'

'If you say so.' Maria didn't sound convinced but she obviously decided not to pursue the subject and left.

Katie took a shower then put on the clean scrubs. She found a plastic bag for her wet uniform then went back to the department to sign out. The day shift had all left now and the night staff were on duty. She checked how Eric Van der Halk was doing and was relieved when she was told that he had been sent to Theatre. The fact that he had got as far as surgery at least meant he had a chance.

She collected her bag from the staffroom then made her way to the exit. Now that the adrenaline had stopped pumping through her veins, she felt completely exhausted and she was looking forward to going home...

'Ah, there you are, Katie. Come along. My car's over here.'

She jumped when Christos suddenly appeared beside her. He had changed into cotton scrubs as well and he looked big and imposing as he stood there in the light from the security lamps. He had obviously showered, too, because his black hair was still damp, curling crisply around his well-shaped head.

Katie swallowed as she tried to work a little moisture into her dry mouth. All of a sudden she was transported back to that moment earlier in the evening when he had held her in his arms. She had felt his body quicken in response to her nearness then, felt her own response to him too, and she was afraid of where it could lead. She couldn't afford to put her heart at risk by falling for him.

The thought came from nowhere and she gasped. Christos's eyes narrowed as he stared at her in concern. 'What's wrong?'

'Nothing.' She dredged up a smile but there was no denying how shaken she felt. She hadn't even finalised her relationship with Petros and here she was, thinking about falling in love with another man. 'It's kind of you to offer me a lift but there's no need. I'll catch the bus as I usually do.'

'It's a reduced service at night.' He checked his watch then shrugged. 'You've just missed a bus and it will be another hour before the next one is due. There doesn't seem much point you waiting around here when I can drop you off on my way home, does there?'

Katie's heart sank. If she refused his offer, it would only make him suspicious and that was the last thing she wanted to do. 'If you're sure it isn't any trouble?'

'It isn't.'

He didn't waste any more time debating the issue as he led her over to his car. Katie slid into the soft leather seat, trying to quell the feeling of panic which filled her. She was tired and stressed so it was understandable that all sorts of crazy ideas should creep into her head, but she mustn't read anything into them. There was no danger of her falling in love with Christos. No danger of her falling in love with any man after what had happened recently. She would be a fool to jump out of the frying pan right into the fire!

They left the hospital and headed into town. It was just gone eight and there was a lot of traffic about. Christos had to slow down when they reached the town centre and that added extra time to the journey. It was a relief when he drew up outside where she lived.

'Thank you for the lift,' Katie said, hurriedly reaching for the doorhandle.

'You're welcome.' He stared up at the darkened windows above the café. 'Do you like living here? It must be very noisy at times, I imagine.'

'It's fine. The room's clean and the rent is reasonable so that's all that matters.'

'But it wasn't what you were expecting when you came here,' he said quietly.

'No, it wasn't.' She turned and looked at him because there was no point pretending. 'I thought I was coming to Cyprus to start a new life with the man I loved. I never imagined I would end up on my own, living above a fast-food restaurant.'

He sighed wearily. 'My cousin has a lot to answer for.'

'Does that mean you believe I was telling you the truth about Petros?' Katie held her breath. Maybe it wouldn't make any real difference to the outcome, but she desperately wanted him to believe in her innocence.

'Yes. I believe you.'

Her heart felt as though it would burst with happiness all of a sudden. 'What made you change your mind?'

'You did.' He captured her hands and held them tightly in his. 'The more I get to know you, Katie, the more convinced I am that you're nothing like the person my cousin described.'

'Thank you.' She was so choked with emotion that she could barely speak, and he sighed.

'There's nothing to thank me for. I behaved appallingly towards you and no amount of apologies will make up for that.'

'It wasn't your fault. You were bound to have believed your cousin. After all, you know Petros and you knew nothing at all about me.'

'Yes, I know him. That's what makes it worse. I should have realised that he is capable of twisting the facts to suit his own ends. If anyone is to blame, it isn't you, Katie. I'm absolutely sure about that.'

Tears rushed to her eyes when he said that. She was so choked with emotion that she couldn't speak. Christos murmured something under his breath as he drew her to him and held her. 'Shh, don't upset yourself now. He isn't worth it.'

Katie wanted to tell him that she wasn't crying because of Petros. She had accepted that Petros had never loved her and all she wanted now was to make him apologise for the way he had treated her. These tears were because it meant so much to her to know that Christos believed in her innocence but the harder she tried to explain that to him, the more muddled up she got.

'It's all right, Katie.' He pulled her closer and dropped a gentle kiss on her forehead. 'I understand.'

Katie froze when she felt the warmth of his lips against her skin. She could feel tingles of sensation spreading from the spot where his mouth had touched and shuddered as she felt the warmth start to spread through every inch of her body. Christos bent and looked at her, his eyes liquid dark in the glow from the dashboard.

'I hate to see you suffering like this. I wish I could turn back the clock and take away all the pain.'

'I wish you could, too,' she whispered, and meant it with all her heart. If she could erase her affair with Petros, she would be free to fall in love, free to do what her heart was telling her to do right now.

He murmured something as he bent to kiss her again. Katie knew that it would be another of those soothing kisses and realised that it wasn't what she wanted. She wanted more than that fleeting brush of his lips against her temple, so much more...

She lifted her face so that their mouths met and felt the ripple of shock that ran through him, yet he didn't pull away as she half expected him to do. Their lips clung for one second, two, before he drew back. He let her go and his face looked strained in the dim light.

'I apologise. That should never have happened,' he said stiffly, and her heart ached when she heard how distant he sounded. 'It's been a stressful day and we're both tired and overly emotional. I don't want you to feel embarrassed about what just happened because there's no need.'

'Of course not.'

Katie opened the door and got out of the car. She thanked him politely for the lift then let herself in and ran up the stairs to her room. She hurried to the window, but Christos had gone by the time she got there, not that she was surprised he hadn't lingered after that kiss.

Turning, she stared around the room, feeling more alone at that moment than she'd felt since she'd arrived on the island. And the worst thing was that it wasn't Petros she wanted right then but Christos. He had apologised for that kiss she had instigated and driven away, and she missed him.

Christos drove straight home after he left Katie. He'd bought the villa on the outskirts of the town three years before because of its spectacular views of the coast. He had wanted to create a home of his own after all the time he had spent living with other people while he'd been growing up. He had spent a lot of money turning it into a haven where he could relax away from the pressures of his job, but he didn't experience the sense of peace he usually did as he drew up. He felt too keyed up and on edge, and it was all down to Katie.

He sighed as he unlocked the front door. Had Katie kissed him first or had he kissed her? He wasn't sure who had been the instigator, not that it mattered. He had been courting trouble the moment he had taken her in his arms. As soon as he had felt her nestling against him he had been overwhelmed with desire. He could no more blame her for that kiss than he could fly to the moon when it was what he had wanted so desperately!

He groaned as he made his way into the sitting room and sank down on the sofa. He had been so sure about his life until he had met her. He had accepted that he had to put his work first and everything else second. But now he found it hard to control all these crazy ideas that kept running riot inside his head, tantalising thoughts about the life he could have with Katie. They could have a wonderful future together. They could have a home, hopefully here on the island, although he would be willing to relocate if it wasn't what she wanted. They could have a family, too, a boy and a little girl who looked exactly like Katie…

Christos took a deep breath as the images in his head spun almost out of control. He had to get a grip on himself and stop all this fantasising. He'd had dreams like this once before, when he'd been going out with Eleni, and they hadn't amounted to anything. Now there was even less chance of him achieving those dreams because he wasn't the man Katie wanted. That honour went to his cousin who had thrown away her love, treated her deplorably, and abandoned her. If he did nothing else, he would make sure that Petros apologised for what he had done to her, so help him!

He went back into the hall and picked up the phone. He knew that his aunt and uncle were away and that Petros was on his own in the villa in the mountains. It was the ideal time to sort this out. He let the phone ring at least a dozen times but there was no reply so he tried Petros's mobile phone next but it was switched off. He left a terse message, asking his cousin to phone him, and hung up.

He would have felt happier if he could have spoken to his cousin but Katie had told him that she'd seen Petros with Eleni that lunchtime so there was no need to worry what he was up to. Maybe Petros had broken his promise to stay away from the town, but spending time with Eleni could only be a good thing. And once the wedding was over, the situation would be less fraught.

The thought did little to soothe him. He knew how hurt Katie was going to be when his cousin got married. He would have done anything in his power to save her from such pain but there was nothing he could do. All he could do was to be there for her afterwards, if she would let him.

It was a big 'if', because Katie might not want anything to do with him once the wedding was over. She might decide to leave Cyprus and that would be the last he saw of her. The thought filled him with dread. He simply couldn't imagine the future without her.

'I wanted to thank you and Dr Constantine for everything you did yesterday. Dylan could have died if you hadn't been there to help him.'

'I take it that he's feeling better today?' Katie smiled at Frank Walters, the father of the little boy who had been admitted with hypothermia following the ferry accident. It was the start of her shift and she'd been on her way to fetch her first patient when Mr Walters had stopped her.

'Much better. The nurse told us that he will probably be discharged this morning after the doctor has seen him,' Fred explained.

'That's wonderful news. It means you'll be able to enjoy the rest of your holiday.'

'We're going home, actually.' He shrugged. 'Amy has been onto the travel agent and asked them to change our flights so we're leaving tomorrow.'

'What a shame. Still, I expect your wife will feel happier once you've got Dylan home.'

'I doubt it. I can't remember the last time Amy was happy about anything.' Fred gave her the ghost of a smile. 'Anyway, if you'd thank Dr Constantine for me, I'd appreciate it.'

'Of course.'

Katie frowned as she watched him walk over to the lift. Obviously, the tension between the couple hadn't lifted. It reminded her of what she'd been thinking the previous day, about there being no guarantees that a relationship would work. It was something she needed to keep at the forefront of her mind, especially after last night.

Kissing Christos like that had been a stupid thing to do. It could have caused untold problems if he hadn't handled it so sensibly. As for getting hung up on the idea that she had missed him, well, that had been crazier still. She was still re-covering from the after-affects of one disastrous relationship without making the mistake of rushing into another!

She tried not to dwell on the thought as she went to collect her first patient, a three-year-old girl called Sophie Angelis. Sophie had been brought in by her mother after complaining of severe abdominal pains. The child was extremely distressed when Katie took them to a cubicle.

'How long has she been like this?' she asked as the mother laid the little girl on the bed.

'About half an hour, maybe a bit longer. I'm not sure exactly when it started,' the mother admitted.

'So you weren't with Sophie when she first started com-

plaining that her tummy hurt?' Katie asked, unfastening the
child's shorts.

'No. I took Sophie into work with me this morning. There
was a pile of emails that had come in through the night and
needed sorting out. Sophie was playing on her own in one of
the villas and a workman came to fetch me because he could
hear her crying.' Andrea Angelis bit her lip as the child let out
a keening wail. 'I don't know what's wrong with her. She was
fine when we left home this morning.'

'Has she been sick?' Katie asked, taking a disposable ther-
mometer out of its packet. She gently inserted it under the
child's tongue but Sophie's temperature was normal.

'Yes, on the way here in the car. I can't understand it
because she's never ill. What do you think is wrong with her?'

'I'll get the doctor to take a look at her.'

Katie left the cubicle. She had a bad feeling about this case
and wanted Christos to see the little girl as soon as possible.
He was leaving Resus but he stopped when he saw her
hurrying along the corridor.

'Do you want me, Katie?'

'Yes. We have a three-year-old child in cubicles and I don't
like the look of her at all,' she explained, determined to behave
in a purely professional manner with him, despite what had
happened the night before.

'What are her symptoms?' he asked, following her lead.

'She's complaining of severe abdominal pain and her
mother says that she vomited on the way here. I've taken her
temperature and it's normal.'

'And she hasn't complained of pain in her abdomen before
today?' he asked as he fell into step with her.

'Apparently not. The mother says that she is never ill and that she was fine when they left home this morning.'

'Hmm. Then we can rule out something like mesenteric lymphadenitis. It's quite common in children and produces symptoms similar to appendicitis—severe abdominal pain and tenderness. However, it's caused by a viral infection and it doesn't sound as though that's the cause in this instance.'

'It could be appendicitis itself,' Katie suggested.

'Yes. Or it could be an attack of colic.' He sighed. 'It could be umpteen different things in fact. That's the problem.'

'What about some kind of toxin which the child might have ingested?'

'It's another possibility, although if it is that, we shall have find out what the substance is as quickly as possible.'

He didn't discount the idea, as many consultants might have done, and she felt her heart lift. It was good to know that he valued her opinion enough to her suggestion seriously. She led the way into the cubicle and introduced him to Sophie's mother.

'Nurse Carlyon told me that your daughter was well when she woke up this morning,' he said as he set about examining the child.

'Yes, that's right. That's why I can't understand what's happened to cause this.' Tears welled into Andrea Angelis's eyes as she looked at her little girl. 'Sophie's never even caught a cold, like most children do.'

'Is it possible that your daughter could have eaten something?' Christos asked. Even though he was being extremely gentle, the little girl had begun to cry in earnest now and Katie hurriedly stepped forward to calm her.

'She had breakfast this morning,' the mother replied uncertainly. 'Just fruit, yoghurt and toast, which is what she always has.'

'And she ate nothing after that?' he persisted, gently palpating the child's abdomen.

Katie could tell that Sophie was loath to have people touching her tummy. 'It's all right, sweetheart,' she said, catching hold of Sophie's hands when the little girl tried to push Christos away. 'I know your tummy hurts but we're going to make you feel better very soon. I promise.'

'No, no!' the little girl shouted, struggling to sit up.

Katie gently eased her back down on the bed, frowning when she smelled the distinct odour of garlic on her breath. The smell was stronger than she would have expected, bearing in mind what Sophie's mother had told them about what her daughter had eaten for her breakfast.

'Nothing since breakfast,' the mother said. 'I know that for a fact because she's been with me all morning.'

'And was she with you all the time?' Christos queried. 'She never left your sight even for a few minutes?'

'Well, no, not all the time,' Andrea admitted. 'I'm a sales rep for a construction firm which has been building some new villas just outside the town. Sophie was playing with her toys in one of the villas. I could see her from my office, though, so I was able to make sure that she didn't wander off,' she added hurriedly.

'Is there anything in the villas which she could have ingested?' He smiled reassuringly when the young mother looked at him in confusion. 'If there's a chance that Sophie could have swallowed some kind of toxic substance, I need to know what it is.'

'You think she's been poisoned!' Andrea exclaimed.

'I don't know. I'm just trying to rule out the various possibilities. The symptoms your daughter is displaying could indicate all manner of things. But if there's a chance that she could have been poisoned then we need to know sooner rather than later.'

'I don't know… I mean, the villas are all empty. Nobody has moved in yet so there's no food in the fridges or in the cupboards.'

'And there's nothing she could have mistaken for food?' Katie put in. 'Young children have such vivid imaginations. That's why so many accidents happen when a child eats or drinks something he mistakes for food.'

'No. Nothing… Oh!' Andrea clapped her hand over her mouth. It was obvious that she'd thought of something.

'What is it?' Christos demanded.

'Rat poison.' The woman was shaking now and could barely speak. 'One of the workmen reported seeing a rat so the foreman put down some pellets.'

'Right.' Christos turned and Katie could see how grim he looked. 'I want her stomach washed out. Ask one of the other nurses to help you. Once we find out what's in those pellets, we'll tailor the treatment accordingly.'

Katie didn't waste any time as she hurriedly left the cubicle. Tina had finished dealing with her patient so she enlisted her help. They collected what they needed and went straight back. Christos was on his way out but he stopped when he saw them and drew Katie aside.

'I'm going to phone the building site and ask the foreman what kind of poison they've been using.'

'I could smell garlic on Sophie's breath just now,' Katie told him quickly. 'It was really strong, too.'

He said something harsh under his breath. 'It sounds like

phosphorous poisoning, then. There's a distinct odour of garlic on the breath if it's been ingested.'

'Can you treat it?' she asked, her heart sinking because it appeared her suspicions had been correct.

'I can try. But there's no guarantee the treatment will work.'

Katie took a deep breath as he hurried away. She had to pull herself together before she went back into the cubicle. She couldn't begin to imagine how Sophie's mother must feel, but it certainly put her own problems into perspective. Maybe she had been hurt and let down but it wasn't the end of her world. She would recover and build a new life for herself. Just for a moment she found herself wondering if Christos would play any part in her future before she dismissed the idea. It was far too soon to be thinking like that.

CHAPTER TEN

'I'M GOING to treat her with sodium bicarbonate in case her liver has been damaged. She'll also need glucose and insulin. I've put the renal unit on standby, too, because her kidneys will need support.'

Christos looked at Katie and could tell that she was as worried as he was about their small patient. His phone call had confirmed that the rodent poison contained yellow phosphorous, a highly toxic substance which was readily absorbed into the body. Yellow phosphorous caused liver, kidney and other major organ failure as well as damage to the central nervous system. The only thing working in Sophie's favour was the fact that her mother had brought her into hospital so promptly. However, the outlook was exceedingly grim.

'What are her chances?' Katie asked quietly.

'Not good. Acute phosphorous poisoning is extremely difficult to treat. Death often occurs within forty-eight hours of the poison being ingested.'

'But she does have a chance,' Katie protested.

'Yes. But it would be wrong to build up the mother's hopes,' he said bluntly.

'It's so awful,' Katie said sadly. 'I hate it when something like this happens. It's always worse when it's a child involved.'

'It isn't easy for any of us, but we have to get over that and do our jobs.' He sighed because he knew how harsh that must have sounded. 'It's not that I don't care. I just can't afford to let my emotions get in the way at the moment.'

'I understand.' She gave him a gentle smile. 'You feel the same way as I do underneath, I expect.'

'Probably.'

Christos turned away. He had always prided himself on his ability to do his job no matter how emotionally taxing it had been. He had rarely allowed anyone to see the effect it had had on him, yet Katie had understood that without him having to explain it to her.

Did she really understand him as well as she appeared to do? he wondered as they made their way to the treatment room. He had no idea, but it made him feel extremely vulnerable just to consider the idea. Even Eleni, whom he had known since childhood, hadn't fully comprehended how distressing his work could be at times. It just seemed to prove what a special relationship he could have had with Katie if circumstances had been different.

The thought was just too difficult to deal with right then when he needed to remain focussed. He pushed it to the back of his mind as they went into the room. Sophie's stomach had been washed out and she was on a drip. She'd been given a mild sedative and that had calmed her down, but she was a very sick little girl. He didn't relish breaking the news to her mother.

Andrea jumped to her feet as soon as she saw him. 'Did you find out what was in those pellets?'

'Yes, and I'm afraid it isn't good news.' He gently sat her

down again in the chair. 'The pellets contain yellow phosphorous, which is highly toxic if it's ingested.'

'But Sophie's stomach has been washed out so that means the poison is out of her body now,' Andrea protested.

'Washing out her stomach will have helped, but some of the poison will already have been absorbed into her body,' he explained.

'But you must be able to do something about it?' Andrea pleaded.

'I can try. But it would be wrong of me to promise you that she will recover. Sophie is a very sick little girl and the next forty-eight hours will be critical. You must prepare yourself for that.'

Andrea broke into a storm of weeping when she heard that. Christos turned to Katie, hating the fact that he couldn't give the poor woman a guarantee that her child would recover. 'Can you take Mrs Angelis to the relatives' room and see that she has a cup of tea, please? It's best that Sophie doesn't see her like this in case it upsets her.'

'Of course.'

Katie put her arm around the young woman as she helped her to her feet. She was the consummate professional as she led Andrea from the room but he knew how hard it was for her to suppress her own emotions. It was hard for him, too, he thought as he turned to the child. He could imagine how he would feel if it was his daughter lying there—

He caught himself up short. His role was to treat the patients, not to wallow in an emotional quagmire of his own making.

'I don't know what I'll do if anything happens to her. I should have kept a closer watch on what she was doing.'

'You mustn't blame yourself. You can't watch over a child

every second of the day.' Katie patted the young mother's arm, wishing there was something she could do to help her. Andrea was beside herself with fear and it was difficult to think of anything that might comfort her. 'Is there someone I can call to be with you? A friend or a relative, perhaps?'

'No. There's no one. It's just me and Sophie.'

'What about Sophie's father?' Katie suggested carefully, not wanting to upset the poor woman any more.

Andrea shook her head. 'He wouldn't be interested even if I knew how to contact him. He's never even seen Sophie. As soon as he found out I was pregnant, he was off like a shot.'

'I see.' Katie sighed. It was awful to think that Andrea was on her own at such a difficult time. It made her see how lucky she was to have her sister. Although she hadn't told Kelly what had gone on since she'd arrived in Cyprus, she knew that her sister was there if she needed her. It just hadn't seemed fair to dump her problems onto Kelly, although she would tell her eventually.

The thought made her more determined than ever to help Andrea. 'Are you sure there isn't anyone you want me to contact?'

'No, there's nobody. My family never wanted me to come here, you see. They warned me that Sophie's father wasn't the reliable type and they were right. They live in Athens and I haven't seen them since I left home. They know about Sophie, but they don't know that I've split up from her father.'

'I'm sure they would want to be here for you, though,' Katie said quietly.

'Maybe. But I'd rather not tell them,' Andrea insisted.

'It's up to you, of course. So there's nobody at all you want me to contact?'

'No... Oh, I suppose I should let my boss know that I'm not in the office.' Andrea bit her lip. 'Nico has been really kind to me—he gave me a job and found me somewhere to live after I had Sophie so I should let him know what's happened.'

'Give me have his phone number and I'll call him for you,' Katie offered, relieved that Andrea had thought of someone at last. She jotted the number on a scrap of paper and stood up. 'See if you can drink some of that tea while I'm gone. You need to keep up your strength for Sophie's sake.'

'Do you think she'll be all right?' Andrea pleaded.

'I don't know.' Katie squeezed her shoulder. 'But if anyone can help her then it's Dr Constantine.'

She left the relatives' room, unsurprised by how much faith she had in Christos. She had worked with a lot of doctors but he stood head and shoulders above them. He was both highly skilled and extremely dedicated and there was no point pretending that she didn't admire him.

Christos's devotion to his work was in complete contrast to the way Petros had viewed his job, too. Although they had worked in different departments, she'd heard rumours about Petros's slapdash approach. She had been too besotted to take any notice of what had been said, but now she found herself comparing the two men. And once again Christos came off best. He was twice the man his cousin would ever be.

Katie was on her way to the canteen for lunch when Yanni stopped her. Sophie had been moved to the renal unit by then; there were indications that her kidneys were failing and she would need dialysis. Katie was desperately hoping that the child would pull through, although she knew that the odds were against her.

'I know you're going for lunch, Katie, so I won't keep you,' Yanni explained. 'I just wondered if you were doing anything on Saturday.'

'Only catching up with all the boring jobs, like washing and ironing.' She smiled at the registrar. 'Why do you want to know?'

'Because I'm having a party on Saturday night to celebrate my engagement,' Yanni told her, blushing. 'Everyone's been invited and I wondered if you'd like to come too.'

'That's really kind of you!' she exclaimed, genuinely touched by his kindness. 'I'd love to come, Yanni. Thank you.'

'Good.' He gave her his address then had to hurry away when Marina came to tell him there was a phone call in the office for him.

Katie made her way to the canteen, thinking about what she would wear for the party. It would be nice to dress up for a change, especially if her colleagues were going to be there. Would Christos be there as well? she wondered as she joined the queue to be served. Yanni had said that everyone had been invited so it seemed likely that Christos would be going. The thought brought a sudden smile to her lips. She couldn't deny that the thought of spending some time with him outside work added an extra dimension to the occasion.

'You're looking very pleased with yourself. What's happened?'

Katie jumped when Maria came up behind her. 'Oh, Yanni has just invited me to his engagement party,' she explained hurriedly, glossing over the real reason why she was looking so happy.

'It should be a good night,' Maria agreed. 'And you have me to thank for it, too.'

'What do you mean?'

'That I'm the one who introduced Yanni to his fiancée. If it hadn't been for me, this party wouldn't be taking place!'

'Oh, I see.' Katie laughed. 'Do you do a lot of matchmaking for your colleagues?'

'Whenever I can,' Maria said airily. 'Mind you, some people are harder to please than others. I'm not sure if even my matchmaking talents can sort out one particular colleague of ours.'

'And who's that?' Katie was only half listening as she tried to decide what she wanted to eat. She opted for a salad in the end and loaded it onto her tray.

'Christos. He definitely needs someone to sort out his love life, or rather the lack of one,' Maria declared as she followed Katie to the till.

'I can't imagine that Christos needs any help in that area,' Katie protested, feeling a sudden spark run along her veins. She had never given any thought to the women in Christos's life yet all of a sudden she found herself consumed by curiosity. Did he prefer blondes or brunettes? Slim women or ones with more curves? Or was he more interested in a woman's personality than in the way she looked?

'Well, he does.' Maria paid for her lunch then led the way to a table in the corner and sat down. 'I can't remember the last time that he went out on a date.'

'Maybe he didn't tell you about it. I mean, he doesn't have to go out with one of the hospital staff. He could be seeing someone from outside work,' she suggested, trying to quell the pang she felt at the thought of Christos dating some unknown woman.

'I suppose so. Although the amount of time he spends at work doesn't leave him much time over to meet anyone else.' Maria sighed. 'That's the biggest problem, of course. He's far too dedicated to his job. It's not surprising that he's still single when he spends all his time working.'

'Maybe he isn't interested in having a relationship,' Katie said, deciding it was time to put an end to the conversation. Speculating about Christos's love life was the last thing she should be doing when she was trying to be sensible.

'Or maybe he hasn't met the right woman yet.' Maria grinned at her. 'You seem to get on really well with him, don't you?'

'Yes, I suppose I do. He's a brilliant doctor and I admire him for that.'

Katie popped a piece of feta cheese into her mouth, wishing that Maria would let the subject drop. Her friend was completely wrong, of course, because she was the last person Christos was interested in. He had made that perfectly clear the previous night after that kiss.

'Sure it isn't more than that?' Maria insisted. 'You just admire him as a colleague, do you?'

'Quite sure.' Katie drummed up a laugh, wanting to put an end to all the speculation once and for all. Knowing that Christos would never see her as anything more than one of Petros's cast-offs was deeply upsetting. 'Believe me, Christos really isn't my type!'

CHAPTER ELEVEN

CHRISTOS paid for his lunch then looked round for somewhere to sit. The canteen was busy that day and there were no empty tables. He suddenly spotted Katie and Maria sitting in the corner and decided that he would join them. Although he usually sat by himself, he would appreciate some company today. What had happened to little Sophie Angelis had hit him hard and it would be good to take his mind off the case for a while.

He had almost reached their table when he heard his name mentioned. He stopped dead, wondering if he should beat a hasty retreat. It was obvious that Katie and Maria hadn't seen him and he didn't want to embarrass them. However, before he could move away, Katie carried on speaking.

'Quite sure.' She gave a cool little laugh. 'Believe me, Christos really isn't my type!'

Christos felt a sudden tightness in his chest. It felt for all the world as though he had suffered a mortal blow, but why? Why did it matter if Katie wasn't attracted to him? He knew that it was Petros she loved and that it was Petros she wanted. Maybe she had kissed him last night but that had been nothing more than an impulse.

He found himself somewhere else to sit, but the food tasted

like sawdust, and after a couple of mouthfuls he pushed the plate away. The hollow ache in his guts was still there despite the fact that he knew how foolish it was to get upset. He'd known the score from the outset, known exactly what his role must be, and nothing had changed. Had it?

His head whirled as all the crazy ideas he'd had recently began to line themselves up into some sort of order. The worrying thing was that they were starting to make a strange kind of sense: was he falling in love with Katie?

The thought brought him to his feet so fast that he almost overturned his chair. He quickly righted it then picked up his tray, took it to the hatch and left. There was a stack of paperwork needing his attention so he would spend the rest of his break dealing with that. As he knew from experience, the best way to deal with any emotional issues was by concentrating on work.

By the time Saturday arrived, Katie was really looking forward to the party. Everyone who wasn't working that night would be there and it promised to be a lot of fun. She would love to know if Christos was going, but she'd seen very little of him for the remainder of the week so there'd been no opportunity to ask him. However, the thought that he might be there that night added a definite sparkle to the occasion.

She had decided to wear a new dress that night, one which she had bought before she'd left England. Made from jade-green silk chiffon, it was the most sophisticated dress she had ever owned. She had imagined herself wearing it when Petros presented her with an engagement ring so in a way it seemed fitting to wear it that night. The funny thing was that she didn't feel sad that it wouldn't be her engagement she would be celebrating. She had accepted what had happened, even though she was determined to make Petros apologise for the way he had treated her.

The party was in full swing when she arrived. Yanni welcomed her warmly and introduced her to his fiancée, Alexia, who worked in the obstetric unit. They spent a few minutes chatting before some more guests arrived. Katie helped herself to a glass of wine then made her way into the garden. Maria immediately spotted her and came hurrying over.

'Katie, how lovely you look!'

'Thank you. So do you.' Katie laughed as she looked around. 'It's amazing how different everyone looks when they're not wearing their uniforms.'

'Not the most flattering of outfits,' Maria agreed as she led her over to where the rest of their group had congregated. There was an almost full turnout that night, with one noticeable exception, Katie realised. There was no sign of Christos so she could only assume that he had decided not to come.

The thought put a bit of a dampener on the evening, although she tried not let anyone see how she felt. Yanni had hired a band and when Takis asked her to dance, she readily accepted. Maria's husband asked her for the next dance so she had no time to mope. It was a traditional Cypriot dance and extremely energetic; she was breathless when it finished.

'No, I can't…really,' she protested when Takis asked her to dance with him again. 'I'll have to sit the next one out while I recover.'

Takis laughed as he went away to find someone else to partner him. Katie walked down the garden until she came to a bench under an old orange tree. It was the perfect spot to cool off so she sat down.

Tipping back her head, she stared at the moonlit sky,

enjoying the feel of the breeze playing over her skin. It was the kind of night she had dreamed of before she'd left England. Petros had been an integral part of those dreams, too, yet she found it difficult to picture his face now. Closing her eyes, she tried to conjure up an image of him. It seemed to work because a face immediately began to form in her mind's eye—chiselled features, crisp black hair, liquid-brown eyes…. She gasped. She may not be able to remember how Petros looked but she could picture his cousin without any difficulty.

She opened her eyes, her heart racing as she stood up. She'd already suffered one major disappointment since she'd arrived on the island and she wasn't about to set herself up for a second one. Christos wasn't interested in her. His only concern was to protect his cousin. The sooner she accepted that, the easier it would be.

Christos had decided not to attend the party in the end. He had managed to get himself back onto a fairly even keel after the upset in the canteen and he was loath to put himself under any pressure again so he phoned Yanni and made his excuses.

He opted to spend the evening at home instead, so after dinner he put a CD in his state-of-the-art entertainment centre. However, after only a few minutes he'd heard enough. Turning off the music, he put a DVD in the player, but it was no better: he couldn't concentrate on the film.

He switched off the machine, wondering how to fill in the rest of the evening. Normally he enjoyed having some time to himself after a busy week, but it wasn't the same that night, and he knew why. He didn't want to be on his own tonight. He wanted to be with Katie.

He sighed. Katie had made it clear that she wasn't interested in him, so why was he still so keen to see her? He knew it was ridiculous but he couldn't help himself. In the end, he decided that he would go to the party but only stay for a short time and then come home. Hopefully, it would help to settle him down.

Yanni was surprised to see him but he accepted Christos's explanation that he'd changed his plans. Once the usual pleasantries had been exchanged, Christos headed out to the garden. Fortunately, everyone was dancing when he got there and they didn't notice him arriving so he was able to find a quiet spot from where he could watch what was going on.

Katie was dancing with a friend of Yanni's and his heart contracted when he saw how lovely she looked that night. He longed to ask her to dance with him but he knew it would be the wrong thing to do. He needed to think about what was happening before he did anything. While there was no doubt in his mind that he was attracted to her, was that all he felt? Or was it possible that he was falling in love with her?

A couple of weeks ago he would have scoffed at the idea but he could no longer rule it out. He certainly felt differently when he was with her. His response to her was far more intense than anything he had experienced before, even with Eleni. But what hope did he have of her ever reciprocating his feelings when she was in love with his cousin?

He groaned, deeply troubled by all the conflicting emotions he felt. He realised that it had been a mistake to come to the party when he was so unsure about his feelings. However, before he could attempt to slip away, Maria saw him and came hurrying over.

'I thought Yanni said you weren't coming tonight?' she exclaimed.

'I managed to make a last-minute change to my plans.' He

glanced at his watch and shrugged. 'It was just a flying visit, though. I can't stay very long.'

'You can't go yet,' Maria declared. 'Not until you've danced with me.'

She didn't give him time to object as she propelled him onto the dance floor. The band struck up again and the next minute everyone was whirling about. They passed Yanni and his fiancée and Christos managed to smile when his registrar asked him if he was enjoying himself. Katie was dancing with Takis and he saw her look at him in surprise when he and Maria danced past.

Christos did his best to behave as though he was having a wonderful time, but every second that passed made him feel increasingly anxious. It would look very strange if he didn't ask the other women to dance with him, and stranger still if he left Katie out. The thought of holding her in his arms made him feel hot all over so that by the time the music stopped he was ready to cut and run, but once again Maria intervened.

'Time to change partners,' she said grabbing hold of Katie and pushing her towards him before she whisked Takis away.

Christos took a deep breath because now he had no choice except to dance with Katie. He took her in his arms, his hand resting lightly on the small of her back, yet he could feel the warmth of her skin scorching his palm. They circled the floor and it soon became apparent from the stiffness of her body how uncomfortable she was.

'I'm sorry if Maria forced you into this,' he said quietly, his heart aching at the thought of how much she must hate having to dance with him after everything that had happened with his cousin.

'I'm sorry too. I'm probably the last person you wanted to dance with tonight.'

'Why do you say that?' he said, his black brows drawing into a heavy frown.

'Because of Petros and everything,' she murmured, avoiding his eyes.

He sighed heavily. 'Look, Katie, what happened between you and Petros was unfortunate. But, as I told you before, I don't believe that my cousin was entirely blameless.'

'Maybe not, but it's bound to have affected the way you see me.'

'It did in the beginning and I won't deny it.' He bent so he could look into her eyes because it was important that he make his feelings absolutely clear on this issue. 'But now that I've had the chance to get to know you, I can see that I was wrong about you.'

'Thank you,' she whispered.

'There's nothing to thank me for,' he said roughly because it was true.

Knowing how much he had hurt her made him feel like the biggest louse alive. He would have done anything to make up for the way he had behaved. They circled the floor once more and his heart lifted when he felt her gradually relax in his arms. When the music changed to a slow waltz, he didn't let her go even though he knew he should. He simply couldn't bear to let her go when he wanted to hold her so much.

He drew her closer, holding her so that her soft curves fitted against the hard contours of his body. His senses seemed to be far more acute all of a sudden. He could feel the softness of her breasts brushing against his chest, smell the scent of her hair, hear the steady rhythm of her breathing, and they were having an effect on him. When they reached a dark section of the garden where there was nobody else dancing, he couldn't resist any longer.

His head dipped as he kissed her with a hunger he couldn't hide. There was a moment when he thought she was going to push him away then all of a sudden she was kissing him back. Her lips clung to his, so soft and sweet that his heart raced into overdrive, beating wildly inside his chest. He was trembling when he raised his head, but so was she. He desperately wanted to kiss her again, but he knew that he mustn't rush things. He would need to make a lot of changes to his life before he could make a proper commitment to her. He certainly didn't want to run the risk of the same thing happening that had happened between him and Eleni. And as for Katie, she needed time to get over Petros... *If* she ever got over him.

A sudden chill enveloped him at the thought. Although Katie had responded to his kiss, it didn't mean that her feelings for Petros had died. Maybe she'd found comfort in his arms, taken solace from the thought that he'd wanted her. There were many reasons why she might have responded to him, but there was no guarantee that she *cared* about him.

The thought filled him with fear. He was falling in love with a woman who might never be able to love him in return.

Katie could feel her heart racing as Christos raised his head. That he should have kissed her with such hunger was too much to take in. However, it was the fact that she had responded with equal fervour which shocked her more. She knew that she needed to work out how she felt because her feelings were far from clear. When the music stopped, she hurriedly put some space between them. People were starting to drift away; there was a buffet supper laid out under an awning and everyone was heading in that direction. Within seconds they were alone.

'Are you hungry?' Christos turned to her and she could see at once how tense he looked. Was he having second thoughts about that kiss, too?

'Not really.' She summoned a smile, but the thought that he regretted what he'd done sent a ripple of apprehension coursing through her. She couldn't bear to think that she was about to make another disastrous mistake.

He frowned when he saw her shiver. 'Are you cold?'

'Just a bit chilly,' she hedged, because she knew that she was on dangerous ground. Christos may have wanted her while they had been dancing but it could have been a purely physical reaction to her nearness. Soft lights, sweet music, a woman in his arms: they were guaranteed to have an effect on a man's libido. However, it didn't mean that he'd wanted *her*.

The thought was so deflating that she shivered again, and he sighed. 'There's no point standing out here while you catch a cold. Come along.'

'Where are we going?' she asked as he led her along the path.

'Inside.' He paused. 'Or we could go back to my house if you prefer.'

Katie didn't know what to say. Even if it was her he wanted, she knew that it was too soon to start another relationship. She needed to bring her affair with Petros to a conclusion before she could move on. Her indecision must have shown on her face because he smiled gently.

'I'm only suggesting that we have a cup of coffee, Katie. Nothing else. You will be perfectly safe if you come home with me.'

'Oh, I see.' She blushed but there was no point denying that she had reservations. 'I just don't think it would be a good idea to rush into anything.'

'Neither do I.' His expression was grave all of a sudden. 'A lot has happened recently and we both need time to adjust. Let's keep things on a strictly friendly footing for now.'

'I think that would be the best thing to do,' she said quietly, wondering if they would be able to stick to it. While neither of them seemed willing to rush into a situation they might come to regret, there was no denying that there was a spark between them.

She sighed as Christos went away to tell Yanni they were leaving. Maybe there was a spark between them but she couldn't make any plans just yet. And when she was free, she didn't intend to jump, head first, into another potential disaster. She intended to think about what she was doing, decide if it was what she really wanted. After all, it was what Christos intended to do.

She frowned as she recalled what he'd said about them both needing time to adjust. Was he still trying to adapt to the idea that she wasn't the kind of woman his cousin had portrayed her to be?

It was the logical explanation, yet she sensed there was something else holding him back. And until she found out what it was, she wouldn't make any plans for the future.

CHAPTER TWELVE

'SHALL we sit outside on the deck? It's quite sheltered out there so you should be warm enough.'

Christos unlocked the sliding glass doors that led to the huge wrap-around deck which encompassed the whole of the first floor of the villa. He still wasn't sure if it had been a good idea to invite Katie back to his house, but now they were here, he intended to stick to his promise. They would have a cup of a coffee and that would be it. However, as he watched her walk to the rail to admire the view, he realised that he was going to have his work cut out. He didn't feel platonic towards her. Anything but.

'It's so beautiful.' She turned and gazed in awe at the black outline of the mountains behind her. 'You've got the sea on one side and the mountains on the other... Wow!'

'You like it?' Christos smiled, delighting in her obvious pleasure. He rarely invited people to his home because he valued the time he spent there on his own. However, her reaction had been everything he could have wished for.

'Like it? I love it!' She smiled at him. 'You are *so* lucky to live in a place like this, Christos. It's the sort of house people dream of owning.'

'I know,' he agreed, going over to stand beside her. 'Not many people can wake up to such fabulous views each morning.'

'Mmm,' she sighed, her gaze still focussed on the mountains.

Christos felt his heart squeeze in an extra beat as he studied the purity of her profile. There was an innate innocence about her that he found irresistible… He swung round, knowing how dangerous it was to allow his emotions to get the better of him if he wanted to stick to his promise. 'I'll make some coffee. Which do you prefer—filter or espresso?'

'Filter, please, otherwise I'll be awake all night.' She smiled at him as she turned away from the view. 'Do you need a hand? And before you politely refuse, I'd better own up and confess that I have an ulterior motive for offering.'

'And that is?' he said, arching a brow.

'I'm dying to see the rest of your house and it's the perfect excuse to go inside and look around!'

'Ah, I see.' Christos laughed as he swept her a mocking bow. 'Be my guest. I'll be in the kitchen if you need me. Just shout if you get lost.'

'Oh, I'm sure I can manage.' She grinned up at him. 'Getting lost is all part of the fun.'

She waggled her fingers at him as she headed along the hall. Christos was still smiling as he made his way to the kitchen. Most people wouldn't have admitted that they wanted to look around but Katie had been quite up-front about it and her honesty was refreshing.

He sighed as he filled the coffee-maker with water. He still hadn't heard from Petros. It was obvious that his cousin was avoiding him but he couldn't keep on doing so indefinitely. After what had happened tonight, it was imperative that they sorted everything out. And when they did so, Christos intended to make his position perfectly clear. Petros had had no right to blacken Katie's name to protect himself.

'Oh, I just love this kitchen. It's fabulous.'

He glanced round when she suddenly appeared. 'Do you think so?'

'Hmm.' Her gaze travelled admiringly over the glossy black-lacquered cabinets and gleaming white marble worktops. 'Everything is so sleek yet so functional. It's nothing like the kitchen Kelly and I had in the flat we rented. That was an absolute nightmare.'

Christos chuckled. 'I have to confess that it was my biggest indulgence when I had the house refurbished. That and the deck, of course. I had that built specially before I moved in.'

'Well, you've done a wonderful job. The whole house is beautiful. I love the fact that everything is so simple and yet so comfortable.'

'That was exactly the look I was aiming for. I can't abide a lot of fuss but I wanted the place to look like a home, not like a showhouse.'

'You've definitely succeeded. I wish I was as good at choosing the right furnishings as you so obviously are.'

'I can't take all the credit for that. I did have help.'

'Did you?' Katie felt her heart sink. Was this the moment when he was going to tell her about the woman who had helped him create such a beautiful home? There had to have been a woman involved, of course. The thing that had struck her most while she'd been looking around was that everything in the house had been chosen with love as well as with care. Had Christos been creating a home for himself and this woman to enjoy together?

'My aunt is an interior designer and she very kindly helped

me.' He shrugged when she looked blankly at him. 'I knew how I wanted the place to look but I didn't have the time to go searching for the right furnishings and fittings so my aunt did it for me.'

'Oh, I see.' Katie could barely contain her relief as she smiled at him. 'Well, you've done a really wonderful job between you.'

'Thank you.' He poured coffee into two china mugs and placed them on a tray along with a bowl of sugar and a jug of cream. 'Where would you like to sit? Inside or out?'

'Out on the deck,' she said immediately, leading the way. There was a glass-topped table and a pair of comfortable rattan chairs outside so she sat down, nodding her thanks when he placed a mug of coffee in front of her. Although it was reassuring to learn that his aunt had been responsible for helping him furnish his home, she still didn't know anything about the women in his life. It was inconceivable that there hadn't been anyone special and for some reason she needed to know what had happened to her.

She took a sip of her coffee then placed the mug on a coaster. 'Have you always lived here on your own?'

'Yes. I moved around a lot after I qualified and even spent some time working in America. I lived in rented accommodation because it was the easy option. When I came back to Paphos, though, I decided it was time I bought a place of my own. It's been great, too. I really enjoy being able to do whatever I want to do when I get home from work.'

'You never get lonely?'

'Sometimes. However, the fact that I don't have to talk to anyone if I don't feel like it makes up for that.' He sighed. 'I expect that makes me sound very unsociable.'

'Not at all,' she said quickly, aware that she had no right to pry like this. She shouldn't be poking her nose into his affairs, yet the desire to find out more about him was too strong to resist. 'I often feel like shutting myself away when I've had a particularly bad day. It's a good job that Kelly understands otherwise we would have ended up arguing all the time.'

'Our work can be extremely stressful,' he agreed. 'It's little wonder that so many relationships break down.'

'A lot of my friends have split up because of the pressure of work.'

'It needs a lot of compromise on both sides to make a relationship work out,' he said quietly.

Katie frowned when she heard the sombre note in his voice. It sounded as though he had been speaking from experience. Had he been in a relationship that had failed because of the pressure of his work? She longed to ask him but she knew she couldn't pry. 'It does,' she agreed, lifting the cup to her lips once more.

He turned to look at her. 'Did you and Petros live together?'

'No.' Katie put the cup back on its saucer. She couldn't help feeling uncomfortable about discussing her affair with him, even though he was under no illusions about what had gone on. 'It wouldn't have been fair to Kelly to ask him to move in with us, and I didn't want to move out and leave her to pay the rent all by herself.' She laughed harshly. 'It was probably the only sensible thing I did, in fact.'

'Don't.' Reaching out he captured her hand. 'You mustn't keep blaming yourself, Katie.'

'But it was my fault. I should have been less gullible.'

'My cousin can be very persuasive when he wants to be.'

Katie frowned when she heard the anger in his voice. Was he angry because of what Petros had done to her or for some other reason? she wondered. Short of asking him outright, she had no way of knowing how he felt, yet she was reluctant to take that step. It was a relief when he changed the subject.

'Do you still intend to see Petros?'

'Yes. I think it's only fair that he accepts responsibility for what he's done.'

'I understand, but is it really worth upsetting yourself?' His hand tightened around hers. 'Wouldn't it be better to put what has happened behind you?'

'I don't think I can. That's why I need to talk to Petros and hear what he has to say.'

'I see.'

Katie shivered when she saw the grim expression on his face as he let her go. She realised that he had completely misunderstood what she'd meant. Christos thought that she wanted to see his cousin because she was hoping they could get back together. However, that couldn't be further from the truth.

'You don't understand,' she said quickly, then stopped when the phone suddenly rang.

'Excuse me.'

He got up and went inside, leaving her alone on the deck. Katie stood up and went to the rail, but this time the view failed to captivate her. She had come within a hair's-breadth of telling him that she no longer loved his cousin but was it true? Surely she needed to see Petros again before she would know for certain how she felt. Granted, she had responded to Christos tonight when he had kissed her, but it didn't prove that she was over his cousin.

It was hard to believe that she might still have feelings for Petros but until she had seen him she couldn't say for certain that she no longer loved him. And she certainly couldn't make any plans for the future.

* * *

'*Yásoo.*'

Christos replaced the receiver on its rest. The call had been from the hospital. There had been a serious accident and Melinda had asked the switch board operator to page him. Yanni should have been on call that night but Christos had offered to cover for him because of the party. He would have to leave immediately and he wasn't sure if he was glad or sorry that it would mean cutting short Katie's visit. Part of him wanted to spend every second he could with her; however, the more rational part was telling him it would be a mistake to get involved when she was still in love with his cousin.

He went back outside to the deck. 'That was the hospital. There's been a serious road accident and I'll have to go into work,' he explained. The thought that Katie might never be able to love him like she had loved his cousin was very hard to accept, but he didn't have a choice. He couldn't *force* her to love him.

'Do you want me to come with you?' she offered, as she followed him back inside.

'No, there's no need. There are enough nurses on duty to cover the accident and anything else that crops up.' He locked up then led the way to his car and opened the door for her. 'I'll drop you off then make my way to the hospital.'

It was only a short drive from his home to the room she rented yet the difference between the two places couldn't have been more apparent. It was Saturday night and the restaurant was packed with people. The noise they were making was tremendous after the peace and quiet at the villa. Christos frowned as he drew up outside.

'Is it always this noisy?'

'It's not too bad during the week, but the weekends can be rather hectic.' She picked up her bag and smiled at him.

'Thank you for showing me around your home. I really enjoyed myself.'

'It was my pleasure.' He cleared his throat because there was no time to dwell on how much he had enjoyed having her in his home. 'I'd better go before Melinda starts to think that I've abandoned her.'

'Of course.'

She got out of the car and crossed the pavement, stepping around a group of young men who were leaving the restaurant. One of the men said something to her but she ignored him as she let herself in. Christos waited until he saw a light come on in the room above before he drove away, but he wasn't happy at the thought of leaving her there. It wasn't the ideal place for her to live if she had to run the gauntlet every time she went home. Maybe he should try to find her somewhere else?

He sighed when it struck him that Katie might not appreciate him interfering. They might have got on extremely well that night but he mustn't make the mistake of thinking it had meant anything. As she had made it clear, her heart still belonged to another man.

The days following the party flew past. Fortunately, nobody seemed to have noticed that she and Christos had left together so there were no awkward questions to answer. It also helped that the department was becoming increasingly busy as more tourists arrived on the island. It meant there was less time to gossip.

Katie was due to start night duty the following weekend so she had a couple of days off in the middle of the week and spent them at the beach. It was bliss to lie on the sand and relax, although she did feel lonely at times. However, it was the perfect opportunity to work out what she was going to do about Petros.

She had been drifting along since she'd arrived in Cyprus but she needed to bring things to a conclusion. She decided that she would find out where he lived and go to see him one afternoon. Hopefully, his fiancée wouldn't be around during the day and they would be able to talk in private. If he would explain why he had behaved the way he had done, then she would be able to put the whole unhappy episode behind her.

She went into work on Friday, ready for her first turn on night duty. Maria worked permanent days so the senior nursing sister on duty was someone Katie hadn't met before. Her name was Ingrid and she told Katie that she was from Sweden, although she had lived on the island for a number of years. She ran the department with brisk efficiency and immediately despatched Katie to the supply room to make a list of what needed replacing.

Katie jotted down the items they needed. She had almost finished when one of the other nurses came to tell her that she was wanted in Paeds Resus. A toddler had been admitted following a fall from a hotel balcony and Christos had requested her help.

Katie handed over the list, somewhat surprised that Christos had asked specifically for her. Although she had seen him on a number of occasions since the party, he hadn't singled her out. She had a feeling that he was keeping his distance after what had happened on Saturday night and couldn't blame him. However, there was no doubt in her mind that he looked pleased to see her when she went into Resus.

The thought gave a definite boost to her spirits as she

hurried over to the bed. 'I believe you wanted me, Dr Constantine.'

'Yes.' He didn't explain why he had requested her help in particular as he turned to the child. 'This is Michael Roberts— a three-year-old who fell approximately ten feet onto concrete. GCS of twelve recorded on site by the paramedics but it's dropped to eight since he arrived. I need to intubate him.'

Katie immediately moved to the head of the bed. The Glasgow coma scale was used to assess the depth of coma or unconsciousness. A patient's GCS was scored between three and fifteen, with three being the worst score and fifteen the best. It was composed of three separate parameters—best eye response, best verbal response and best motor response. A GCS of thirteen or above indicated a mild brain injury, nine to twelve a moderate injury, and eight or less a severe brain injury. The rule in emergency care was less than eight, intubate.

She handed Christos the laryngoscope and an appropri- ately sized breathing tube. Paeds Resus was supplied with equipment especially suited for use with young children so ev- erything was on hand. Once the tube was inserted, she taped it in place.

'I need to assess the full extent of his injuries,' Christos said crisply. 'He's going to need surgery, though, so can you phone the neurosurgical registrar and put him on standby?'

'Do you want me to book him in for a scan as well?' she asked.

'I think an MRI in this instance.' He frowned. 'The neuro- surgeons will need a full picture of what they're dealing with so we'll get it done right away. Tell the MRI technician that I shall authorise it.'

'Of course.'

Katie made the calls, thinking how wonderful it was to have such facilities so readily available. Where she had worked before, an MRI scan needed to be booked in advance and there was usually a quibble about the cost before it was sanctioned.

'Everything set up?' Christos asked when she went back to the bed.

'Yes. The MRI scanner is available whenever you need it and the neurosurgical reg said to tell you that he will meet you there.'

'Good.' He straightened up and she saw the concern in his eyes. 'This little chap is going to need all the help he can get.'

'It's a serious injury?' she said, glancing at the small figure lying on the bed.

'Very serious.' His tone was sombre. 'His skull's been fractured above his left ear. A child's skull is far more malleable than an adult's so that's something in his favour. But even if the bone hasn't splintered, there's bound to have been severe jarring which could cause extensive swelling to the brain. The sooner he's in Theatre the better, but we need to get the basics done first. I need to have a word with the parents so will you accompany him to the MRI unit and stay with him?'

'Of course.'

'Thank you, Katie.'

He gave her a quick smile but that didn't lessen its impact in any way. As Katie went to the phone to request a porter to help her, she found herself smiling, too. There seemed to be a little bubble of happiness lodged in her chest, just waiting its chance to expand. However, until she had spoken to Petros it would have to remain as it was. She wasn't free yet to start hoping there might be a happy-ever-after. But she would be. Soon.

CHAPTER THIRTEEN

'THERE'S an area of bleeding just here. We'll need to deal with that first of all.'

'Of course.' Christos nodded as his colleague from the neurosurgical department pointed to one of the dozen or so images that were being displayed on the monitor screen.

They were standing in the viewing area outside the room where the MRI scanner was sited. He had asked Katie to stay with them while the scan was being done because he knew that Michael's parents would be glad of her support. He had specifically requested her help because of the rapport she established so quickly with any relatives. He glanced at her and wasn't surprised when he saw that she had a comforting arm around the child's mother. It was so typical of her caring attitude, and yet more proof of how stupid he'd been to believe his cousin's lies.

'Will you take the child straight to Theatre?' he said, returning his attention to the case before he got sidetracked.

'Yes. There are definite signs that pressure is building up inside his skull and I don't want there to be any delay. The sooner we stop that bleeding, the better his chances will be. Maybe you would have a word with his parents for me while I get ready?'

'Of course. Leave it with me,' Christos agreed.

He went over to the parents as the other man hurried away. Now that the scan had been completed they were able to leave the viewing room. He led them into the corridor and sat them down on some chairs. There was nobody about and it was as good a place as any to talk.

'My colleague from the neurosurgical department was able to study the scan while it was being done,' he explained. 'He's going to operate on Michael to remove a blood clot that has formed inside his skull.'

'Will he be all right after that?' the child's father asked anxiously. 'I mean, just the same as he was before the accident happened?'

'I'm afraid I can't give you a guarantee as to the outcome, Mr Roberts,' he said quietly. 'A serious head injury like this can cause permanent physical and mental disability, and we have no way of knowing how much damage has been done to your son's brain at this stage.'

'I don't know how it happened,' the mother wailed. 'One minute Michael was playing on the balcony with his toy cars and the next there was this awful scream!'

Christos sighed when she started to sob. There was very little comfort he could offer her in a situation like this. He decided to stick to practicalities instead. 'Michael will be taken straight to Theatre after he leaves here. You are welcome to go with him and wait there. Nurse Carlyon will show you the way.'

He beckoned Katie over as the young couple clung together. 'See if you can find out the name of anyone they would like us to contact, would you? It's going to be a very difficult time for them and they will need all the support they can get.'

'Of course.'

She gave him a quick smile before she went back to the couple. Christos watched as she escorted them to the lift then made his way back to the trauma unit. Yanni was on duty that night and he would have thought it very odd if his boss had offered to trade places with him.

Christos suppressed the urge and left, knowing how ridiculous it was to hang around until Katie came back. He was acting like a love-sick teenager and he was way past the stage of being that! He drove home and made himself some supper. He wasn't really hungry but it helped to fill in the time. Normally, he looked forward to his evenings off, but the thought of being on his own that night was less than appealing. Maybe it would be the ideal time to go and see Petros? His cousin wouldn't expect him to turn up at this time of the night and he would have the advantage of surprise. It might help him get at the truth.

His stomach was churning as he got into his car. In another hour, he was sure that he would have all the proof he needed of Katie's innocence. Just for a moment, he found himself wondering what effect it would have on Eleni before he consoled himself with the thought that there was no need for her to find out. He and Petros would sort this out between them, although he wasn't sure what would happen after that. It all depended on Katie. If she was still in love with his cousin, he had to accept that. But if there was a chance that she might get over Petros in time then he intended to be there for her. He would wait as long as he had to if it meant they could be together.

The rest of Katie's shift passed without incident. Although there was a steady stream of minor injuries that needed attending to, it was very low key after the frenetic pace of a Friday night in central Manchester.

She went home to bed and managed to sleep for a couple of hours, but she was wide awake again by eleven a.m. She had a shower then sat by the open window to eat her breakfast. It was another glorious day, a gentle breeze offering a welcome relief from the heat of the sun, but she had no intention of spending the day at the beach. Today was the day she intended to see Petros. The longer she put it off, the harder it would be, so she would get it over with.

She dressed in cotton jeans and a white T-shirt then went down to the café. She needed Petros's address and she was hoping that her landlord would help her find it. She had ruled out the idea of requesting the information from the hospital. Hospitals were loath to hand out information about their staff, and she hadn't wanted to arouse people's suspicions by asking for it. Petros must be listed in the local phone directory, though, and with her landlord's help she should be able to trace him through that.

Ten minutes later, she had the information she needed. Petros lived on the outskirts of Paphos so she left the café and went to the taxi rank. Although she knew exactly what she wanted to say to him, she had no idea how he would react when she appeared at his door. By the time the taxi dropped her off outside the house, she felt sick with nerves, but she was determined to go through with it.

Katie knocked on the door. She could hear music coming from inside so obviously someone was in. She steeled herself when the door opened but oddly enough she felt remarkably little when Petros appeared. It was hard to believe that this man had once meant the whole world to her.

'Hello, Petros,' she said quietly.

'Katie!' All the colour drained from his face as he stared at her. 'How did you find out where I live?'

'From the telephone directory.' She smiled thinly. 'You never did give me your address. I should have realised why at the time.'

A wash of colour ran up his face. 'Look, Katie, I don't know what you hope to achieve by coming here,' he began.

'Not a lot. I just feel that you owe me an explanation.' She stared pointedly at the door. 'Are you going to invite me in, or shall we talk out here where everyone can hear what's going on?'

'You'd better come in,' he said grudgingly, stepping aside.

'Thank you.' Katie followed him into the hall and waited while he closed the front door.

'Through here,' he said, leading the way through the house to a room at the back which overlooked the garden. Although the place was expensively furnished, it was far too showy for her taste and lacked the simple charm of Christos's home. It was rather like its owner, she thought: all show and very little substance.

'This is a complete waste of time.' Petros plonked himself down on a sofa. He looked rather like a petulant child who had been caught doing something naughty. 'I'm sorry that you've had a wasted journey, but if you're hoping we can get back together then I'm afraid it's not going to happen. Surely my cousin told you that I am getting married?'

'Yes, he did. It's a shame you didn't tell me that yourself.' Katie gave him a cool look as she sat down. 'How did you happen to overlook such an important fact, Petros? I mean, you never even *hinted* that you were seeing someone, let alone told me that you were engaged to be married.'

'I wasn't engaged then,' he replied with breathtaking arrogance. 'Eleni and I only got engaged when I returned to Cyprus.'

'But you were still in a relationship. Did it never occur to you to mention that to me?'

'There was no point. It wasn't as though we were serious about one another.'

'It was serious enough for us to sleep together,' she pointed out.

He shrugged. 'It isn't a big deal for most people.'

'Well, it was a big deal for me. You must have known that I would never have slept with you if I'd had any idea that you were involved with another woman.'

He leant forward in his seat. 'It was just a bit of fun, Katie—surely you knew that.'

He smiled beseechingly at her, just like he had done when he had begged her to go out with him. The difference now was that she understood what he was like and she wasn't going to be taken in a second time.

'So it was never more than a bit of fun for you, even though you told me that you loved me?'

His smile disappeared in a trice. 'It was what you expected me to say. You were such a little prude that you would never have slept with me otherwise.'

'And that's your excuse, is it? You told me that you loved me so I would sleep with you?'

He didn't say anything to that—just shrugged. Katie could barely contain her anger. 'So why didn't you tell me all this before you left Manchester? I would never have flown over here if you'd told me the truth.'

'Because I thought you would realise it was the end of our affair. Most women would have done. They wouldn't have needed the message hammered home like you did.' He glared at her, dropping any pretence at civility. 'I was stunned when you phoned me up and told me that you'd booked your flight and that you were moving here.'

'So instead of being honest and admitting what you'd done, you ignored my calls after that. And, as if that wasn't bad enough, you then had the nerve to tell Christos that I had been hounding you!' She shot to her feet and glared at him. 'You really are despicable, Petros.'

His face darkened as he rose as well. 'None of this would have happened if you hadn't been so naïve. Just because a man sleeps with a woman, it doesn't mean that he wants to spend his life tied to her.'

'Obviously not where you are concerned it doesn't,' she retorted, realising how foolish she'd been to hope that he would apologise. 'I just hope your fiancée knows what you're like otherwise she is going to end up disappointed. Fidelity isn't a word you understand.'

'You and my cousin have a lot in common. He shares your idealistic view of the world, too.' He laughed scornfully. 'He's not had much luck with women in the past but you two seem ideally suited to me.'

Katie had no idea what he meant about Christos not having had any luck with women, but it wasn't the right time to worry about it. She had done what she had set out to do and if it had achieved nothing else, at least she had made her feelings clear.

Petros didn't bother accompanying her to the door so she let herself out. There was a taxi dropping off a fare at the top of the road and she asked the driver to take her back to the town centre. And on the way there she thought about what she intended to do next.

There was nothing to keep her in Cyprus now. She could return to England or find a job somewhere else. Even though she hadn't received an apology from Petros, she was ready to put the past behind her and look to the future…wherever that might lie.

She sighed. It wasn't the thought of where her future might lie that troubled her, but who would play a part in it. Although she hoped that Christos would be around, there were no guarantees. He might be happy for her to leave once he found out that she no longer posed a threat to his cousin.

Christos could hardly contain his frustration when he went into work the following day. His attempts to track down his cousin had been a complete waste of time. Petros hadn't been at the villa in the mountains and it had been too late by the time he'd driven back to town to check if his cousin had been at his own house. It would be another day at least before he could sort out this mess and it was hard to accept another delay.

He threw himself into his work in the hope that it would distract him. Happily, the news from the neurosurgical department about Michael Roberts was extremely positive. The blood clot had been removed and the child was stable. At least that had been one success. By the time he was ready to leave work that night, he was feeling far more positive. He would track down his cousin somehow, so help him.

He was on the point of leaving when Katie arrived for her shift and he stopped to speak to her, using the excuse of updating her about Michael's progress. She smiled in delight when he told her that the child had responded well to the treatment he'd received.

'That's wonderful news. His parents must be so relieved.'

'They are.' Christos felt a rush of happiness fill him. Just seeing her smile like that made the world seem a better place. Maybe he hadn't managed to sort everything out but he would do so soon, he thought, smiling at her. 'How did you get on after your first turn on night duty? Did you manage to get some sleep?'

'A couple of hours.' She lowered her voice when she saw Yanni leaving one of the cubicles. 'I went to see Petros this afternoon.'

'You did?' It was impossible to hide his dismay, and she sighed.

'Yes. I know you didn't want me to go and see him, Christos, but I had to.'

'And did it help?' he asked, his heart thumping as he wondered what had happened. He couldn't bear to think of her falling under Petros's spell a second time, but he knew how persuasive his cousin could be.

'Yes, it did. It helped enormously.'

'I'm glad,' he said quietly, trying to assess her mood. She didn't seem to be angry or upset so did that mean she had forgiven his cousin, or that she no longer cared about him? The uncertainty of not knowing how she felt was the hardest thing of all. 'So, did Petros apologise?' he asked, trying to keep a tight rein on his emotions.

'Oh, no! He doesn't believe that he did anything wrong.' She shrugged. 'It doesn't matter any more. Just seeing him again helped me put everything into perspective.'

'So what do you intend to do now?' he asked, hoping she couldn't hear the fear in his voice. Now that there was nothing to keep her in Cyprus, she would leave, and he didn't know how he was going to bear it.

'I'll probably go back to England, although I'm not sure

if I'll stay there. My plans are very much up in the air at the moment.'

'You can stay on at the hospital for as long as want to,' he offered hurriedly, desperate to win himself a little extra time.

'Thank you. It's kind of you to offer, but it could prove difficult when Petros returns to work after the wedding.'

Meaning that it would be upsetting for her to be constantly reminded that his cousin had chosen someone else?

Christos's heart sank when he realised that she must still be in love with Petros. 'You must do whatever is best for you, Katie,' he said quietly.

'I shall.' She gave him a wistful little smile then went to sign in. Christos collected some files from his office and drove home. He made himself a pot of coffee and settled down to work on some case reviews, hoping it would help if he concentrated on other people's problems instead of his own. After all, his life was essentially the same. He still had his job and that had been enough to keep him going in the past. However, in his heart he knew that work wouldn't be enough this time. This time he had even more to lose: Katie and that future he had only just dared to dream about. He couldn't imagine how hard it was going to be to carry on without her.

CHAPTER FOURTEEN

KATIE went to the travel agent's office the next day and made arrangements to fly home to England the following Saturday. There wasn't any point her staying in Cyprus now. If Christos had wanted her to stay, he would have told her so last night. He was probably relieved that she was leaving and the thought was very difficult to accept.

She got through her last stint on night duty and had the following two days off. She went to the beach again but even though the weather continued to be glorious, she derived no pleasure from lying on the sand. She kept thinking about the mess she had made of her life, and how hard it was going to be to pick up the pieces when her heart wasn't in it. She wanted to stay here with Christos, wanted time to allow these precious new feelings to develop. Deep down she knew that they could have had something truly special together.

In an effort to stave off a bad case of the blues, she decided to eat in the café that night. Stavros, her landlord, made a huge fuss of her when she appeared. He found her a table near the window and gave her a complimentary half-bottle of wine to drink with her meal. He seemed genuinely upset when she told him that she was leaving at the weekend and that made her feel worse. She was going to miss Cyprus and the people she'd met there so much.

The café soon got busy. Katie was aware that she was occupying a table for four and didn't linger over her meal. She paid the bill and thanked Stavros for the wine, intending to go straight back upstairs. However, when she got out into the street, she discovered that there was a crowd of youths gathered on the pavement.

'Excuse me,' she said, trying to ease past them.

'Where are you off to?' One of the young men grabbed hold of her around the waist. 'Why don't you come and have a drink with us, darling?'

'No, thank you.' Katie tried to free herself but he wouldn't let her go.

'That's not very nice, is it? I offer you a drink and you turn your nose up. You should try being a bit more friendly.'

'I don't want a drink,' she said firmly. 'Now, please, let me go.'

'And what if I won't? What are you going to do then, eh?' He grinned as his friends started to jeer. 'Tell you what—I'll let you go if you give me a kiss. I can't say fairer than that, can I?'

'Stop it!'

Katie wedged her hands between them as he bent towards her and shoved him away. He swore loudly as he made a lunge for her, but instead of grabbing hold of her, as he'd intended to do, he pushed her over. Her head hit the pavement with a sickening thud and everything started to spin. She could hear people shouting but she was so dizzy from the impact that she had no idea what was going on. It was only when she recognised Stavros's voice that she realised he had chased the youths away.

Stavros helped her to her feet and took her back into the café. He insisted on calling an ambulance and stayed with her until it arrived. Katie tried to explain that she didn't need to go to hospital but the paramedics insisted that she must be checked over, and in the end it was too much effort to refuse. She sighed as they helped her into the ambulance. She only hoped that none of the staff who knew her were on duty that night.

Christos hadn't been rostered to work that night but he'd stayed on to deal with a patient who was exhibiting all the signs of a triple A—an abdominal aortic aneurysm. It was a medical emergency because of the risk of the aneurysm rupturing. Once he had established what the problem was, he sent the patient to Theatre for arterial reconstructive surgery. He was getting ready to leave when Katie was brought in by the ambulance.

'What happened?' he demanded as the paramedics wheeled her into a cubicle.

'There was a scuffle outside the restaurant and I fell over,' she explained. 'I hit my head on the pavement, but I'm fine.'

'Did you lose consciousness?' he asked, bending down so he could examine the bruise on her left temple.

'No. I saw stars for a moment but I didn't black out.' She bit her lip as he delicately probed the skin. 'That really hurts.'

'No wonder,' he said gruffly, straightening up. 'You've taken quite a knock. It's going to need a few stitches but we'll sort that out after you've had a CT scan.'

'Oh, there's really no need for a scan. It was just a bang on the head—nothing major.'

'Leave me to be the judge of that.'

He sighed because he knew how harsh that must have

sounded, but he was afraid that his emotions would run away with him. He told the nurse to take Kate to the radiology unit. It would take at least half an hour before the scan was ready and he must use the time to get himself together. However, as he watched the nurse wheel Katie along the corridor, he knew how difficult it was going to be to treat her like any other patient when she meant so much to him.

By the time Katie came back from her scan, Christos had managed to get a grip on himself. There was no sign of any damage to her skull so it was a case of stitching up the cut. He opted to do the suturing himself rather than ask someone else to do it. Once he'd administered some local anaesthetic to numb the area, he set to work, trying to ignore the effect her nearness was having on him.

'How many stitches are you putting in?'

'Four should be sufficient. Don't worry. I'll make sure they don't leave a scar.'

'Thank you.' She took a quick little breath then hurried on. 'I booked my flight this morning. I'm going back to England on Saturday.'

'You were lucky to get a seat,' he said as evenly as he could when it felt as though a giant hand was crushing his heart. 'Most flights are booked up months in advance at this time of year.'

'It was a cancellation so I was lucky to get it. There doesn't seem any point staying on here now, though.'

'No. I'm sure there doesn't.'

Christos made the last tiny stitch then cut the thread, hoping she couldn't tell that his hands were trembling. The thought that she would be leaving in a few days' time was more than he could bear. He wanted to beg her to stay but how could he when it wasn't him she loved but his cousin? It took every scrap of strength he possessed not to let her see how devastated he felt.

'Try to keep the stitches dry and they should heal quite quickly.'

'Thank you.' She gave him a tight little smile. 'I'm sorry to be such a nuisance. You should have gone home by now and I've held you up.'

'It doesn't matter.' He dropped the needle into the sharps box and peeled off his gloves. 'I'll run you home. It will save you having to find a taxi.'

'Are you sure? I don't want to take you out of your way...'

'You aren't,' he said curtly, because he was in no mood to argue. He signed her notes and gave them to the admissions clerk. Katie waited until he finished then followed him outside, nodding her thanks when he helped her into the car. She sighed as she settled back in the seat.

'I'll be a lot more sympathetic from now on when I treat someone who's had a bang on the head. My head is thumping. It feels as though there's a whole orchestra tuning up inside my skull.'

'A couple of painkillers should sort out any residual headache,' he said. 'Plus you'll feel a lot better after a night's sleep.'

'If only.' She grimaced. 'This is one night when I could do without all the noise from the restaurant.'

Christos turned and looked at her. 'You can always stay at my house, if you want to,' he said, wondering if he was mad to suggest it. She was leaving on Saturday so surely he should be keeping his distance, instead of making life more difficult for himself? However, he couldn't bear to think of her having to put up with a lot of noise when she was feeling ill.

'Oh, I wouldn't dream of putting you to so much trouble.'

'You're not.' He shrugged, feigning an indifference he wished he felt. 'The guest room is ready so it's not as though I'm going to have to set to and start making up a bed for you.'

'It would be lovely to have some peace and quiet,' she admitted wistfully.

'Then think about staying at my house tonight.'

He started the engine, knowing it would be wrong to try and persuade her. It was up to her to decide if she trusted him enough to stay the night. They left the hospital and drove towards the town until they came to the main road. Christos drew up by the kerb and glanced at her.

'So which is to be? Back to your home or to mine?'

She bit her lip and he could tell how undecided she was. He had already prepared himself for a refusal when she said quickly, 'Yours. I'll take you up on your offer if you're sure you don't mind.'

'I don't mind a bit, Katie,' he said truthfully, as he set off again. He took a deep breath, trying to batten down the feeling of euphoria which filled him, but it was impossible. Maybe it was only a small step but it was one which might lead to many others.

'Why don't you sit on the deck while I make us something to drink?' Christos unlocked the doors and pushed them open. 'I won't be long so make yourself at home.'

'Thank you.'

Katie took a deep breath as she walked out onto the deck. Night had fallen now and it was pitch dark outside. She could see the harbour lights in the distance, twinkling like strings of precious jewels against the velvet-soft sky. The scent of lemons carried on the breeze from the trees in the garden. It was a night just made for romance but she mustn't think about that. It was too dangerous in her present state of mind.

Why had she accepted Christos's invitation to stay here? she wondered as she sat down on a chair. She was leaving in a few days' time so what was the point of hoping for something that was never going to happen? She was only setting herself up for more heartache when she should have learned her lesson from recent experiences. However, she didn't regret her decision. At least she would have these few hours alone with him to look back on after she'd left.

'Here you are. I decided it would be safer to avoid alcohol after that bump you've had so it's just fresh orange juice and soda water.'

'It looks delicious,' Katie said as he placed two tall glasses, tinkling with ice, on the table. She took a sip of the drink and sighed appreciatively. 'It tastes delicious, too.'

'Good.' He pulled out a chair and sat down. 'How's your headache now? I have some paracetamol if you need it.'

'It's starting to ease off. I'll wait and see if it will settle down on its own.' She smiled rather ruefully. 'I hate having to take medication, even something simple like paracetamol. Stupid, isn't it?'

'Not at all. I wish more people were wary about over-the-counter remedies. They don't realise the harm they can do to themselves by taking them.' He grimaced. 'Sorry. You definitely don't need a lecture tonight.'

'I don't mind.' She laughed when his brows rows. 'It's true. I enjoy talking about medical matters.'

'You're just being kind.'

'I'm not! Honestly, Christos, I wouldn't say it if I didn't mean it. I certainly wouldn't lie to *you*.'

She didn't realise how vehement she'd sounded until she saw his eyes darken. She picked up her glass again, praying that he would let the comment pass. What could she say if he asked her why she wouldn't lie to him in particular? That she cared too much about him not to tell him the truth?

'I would never lie to you either, Katie. You deserve to be told the truth more than anyone I know.'

His deep voice grated and she shivered when she heard the emotion it held. When he placed his glass on the table, she jumped. The sound of glass striking glass seemed to reverberate inside her like the drum roll that preceded a major event. She was actually holding her breath as she waited for him to continue.

'I care about you a great deal, Katie. I know you probably don't want to hear me say this, but I need to tell you how I feel.'

Katie felt her heart shudder to a stop. 'You *care* about me?' she whispered, wondering if the bump on her head had affected her hearing.

'Yes.' He captured her hand and raised it to his lips. 'I care about you very much.'

Katie closed her eyes as a wave of happiness flooded through her. It was hard to believe that she wasn't dreaming but the proof was the fact that she could feel him gripping her hand. 'I care about you, too,' she murmured.

She heard him take shuddering breath and opened her eyes, feeling her heart race when she saw the way he was looking at her. When he stood up and gently pulled her to her feet, she didn't hesitate. She wanted him to prove how much he cared more than she had wanted anything in her life.

His lips were hungry as they took hers in a kiss that seemed to reach deep into her very soul. Katie clung to him as the kiss transported them both to dizzying heights. His breathing was ragged when he drew back but so was hers—just as uneven.

'I swore I wouldn't rush you, but I can't help myself. Forgive me, Katie, but I want you so very much.'

'I want you, too,' she said, her voice trembling as the enormity of what was happening hit her.

He took her into his arms again and this time his kiss was as tender as the first one had been passionate. Katie knew that he was trying to show her by actions as well as by words how much he cared.

She kissed him back without any hesitation because there was no need to wonder if she was doing the right thing—she knew she was. She cared about him, too, cared about him and loved him as well.

The thought seemed to explode inside her in a shower of stars and she gasped. Christos drew back and looked at her in concern.

'What is it? What's wrong?'

'Nothing.' She kissed him on the mouth, let her lips cling for a moment, then smiled at him. 'Everything is perfect.'

His eyes bored into hers for a moment and what he saw there obviously reassured him. He pulled her back into his arms and rained kisses over her face. Katie sighed with pleasure as she felt his lips brush her cheeks, her nose, her jaw. Everywhere his mouth touched, her skin tingled. When he drew back she frowned because she didn't want these delicious kisses to stop.

He laughed softly. 'Maybe we should call a halt. After all, you did say that you had a headache.'

'Yes, but it's gone now.' She smiled up at him, loving the

fact that he could tease her this way. 'You seem to have found
the perfect way to cure it, Christos.'

'That's good to hear.' He rewarded her with another linger-
ing kiss. 'I could suggest a way to make sure it doesn't come
back, but it depends how you feel about the treatment I would
like to prescribe.'

'I'm happy to place myself in your capable hands, Doctor,'
she said demurely.

'Really? Then I think I shall take that as my answer.'

Bending down, he lifted her into his arms and carried her
indoors. Katie wound her arms around his neck, enjoying the
powerful strength of his body as he carried her along the
hall. He stopped at the bottom of the stairs and she smiled
wickedly at him.

'You can put me down if I'm too heavy for you.'

'You're not too heavy.' He kissed her softly on the mouth.
'You are perfect, Katie. In every way.'

'Thank you,' she whispered, her heart overflowing with
happiness as he carried her up the stairs. She knew what he
was telling her, of course. That no matter what had happened
when they had met, he no longer believed that she was the
kind of woman she had been portrayed as.

The thought seemed to unlock the very last of her inhibi-
tions so that when he laid her on the bed, she could feel herself
trembling with desire. He didn't bother turning on any lights
as he sat down beside her but she didn't need light to know
how he was looking at her. Maybe he hadn't told her in so
many words that he loved her, but she could tell how he felt
and that was enough.

Reaching up, she cupped his cheek with her hand. 'Make
love to me, Christos.'

'If you're sure it's what you want,' he said, turning his head so that his warm breath clouded on her palm.

'It is,' she said simply, because there was no point pretending. She wanted him and he wanted her, and there was no reason why they shouldn't be together. What had happened in the past was over and this was their time now.

He framed her face between his hands. 'It's what I want more than anything, Katie.'

There was such conviction in his voice that she knew she was right: he did love her. But before she could say anything, he kissed her with a passion that left her breathless. What little experience she had of love-making hadn't prepared her for the feelings that were running riot inside her at that moment. She knew that she had to tell him that because it was important he understand how much this meant to her. When he drew back, she looked straight into his eyes.

'I've never wanted anyone as much as I want you, Christos.'

An expression of awe mingled with relief crossed his face when he realised what she was telling him. Katie drew him down to her and kissed him, letting loose all the feelings that had been building inside her. She had never really known how to please a man before but it was different now. When she opened her mouth so they could deepen the kiss she heard him gasp, and when she ran her hands down his back she felt him tremble. Was it love that had taught these wonderful new skills? She knew it was true and it just seemed to prove that what they were doing was right. She and Christos were meant to be together.

'Katie, Katie.' He murmured her name as he rained kisses over her face and jaw. His mouth skimmed down her throat until it reached the collar of her blouse. He drew back, holding her gaze as he began to undo the buttons. Katie could feel the tension building inside her as he worked his way down the row until he came to the very last button of all.

'If you're not sure about this, tell me to stop,' he whispered urgently.

'It's what I want, Christos. I'm absolutely sure about that.'

He kissed her quickly on the lips then undid the final button and parted the front of her blouse. All she had on underneath was a pale blue lace bra and she heard him draw in a shuddering breath as he looked at her.

'You are even more beautiful than I imagined,' he said huskily.

Katie shivered. The fact that he had imagined how she would look seemed to have set light to her own passion. She sat up and shrugged off her blouse then undid his shirt, her hands trembling as she parted the front of it. His chest was broad and well muscled, the sprinkling of black hair that covered his pectoral muscles clinging to her fingers when she pressed her palms against him. His skin felt so warm, so vital that she closed her eyes so she could savour the feel of it.

He whispered something in his own language as he laid her back against the pillows. Then, with infinite care, he ran his hands over the swell of her breasts, mimicking the way that she had touched him. Katie could feel her nipples hardening as he caressed her but she didn't care if he could see what was happening to her. She wanted him and she wasn't ashamed of her desire.

'So beautiful,' he murmured again, as he eased the strap of her bra off her shoulder. He pushed the lace cup aside and stroked her nipple with his thumb until it was hard and taut. Only then did he replace his fingers with his mouth, drawing on the rosy nub until she moaned in pleasure. He raised her slightly while he undid the hooks on the back of her bra then repeated the process with her other breast, wringing more moans from her. Shrugging off his shirt, he lay down beside her and pulled her to him so that she could feel how aroused he was, too.

'I want you so much, Katie,' he whispered, interspersing the words with butterfly-soft kisses.

'I want you too,' she whispered back, bending so that she could kiss his throat and then his chest. Her mouth slid over his warm skin until she reached his nipple and gently began to tease it with her tongue, smiling when she heard him groan. 'If it's hurting you, I can stop.'

'Oh, it isn't pain I'm feeling, believe me,' he growled, his hand sliding into her hair. He gently tugged on her hair until she lifted her head then kissed her hungrily. 'I don't think I have ever felt this way, Katie. Every bit of my body and my soul is aching for you.'

It was so exactly how she felt that her heart overflowed with happiness. She was already reaching for him when he reached for her. The rest of their clothing was soon dispensed with and then there were no more barriers between them, neither physical nor mental ones. When Christos entered her, Katie knew everything that had happened before this moment no longer counted. *This* was the first time she had made love. *This* was the first time that she had ever truly been in love.

CHAPTER FIFTEEN

CHRISTOS knew he would remember that night until the day he died. When Katie fell asleep in his arms, he stayed awake. He didn't want to miss a single second of this time he had with her by sleeping. When dawn started to creep across the sky, he found himself wishing that he could stop the clock. He didn't want this magical night to end.

Pale fingers of light were filtering into the room when she stirred. Christos waited with his heart in his mouth. This was the true test, of course, the moment when he would discover if she regretted what they'd done. In the light of day, she might change her mind, wish that she hadn't slept with him...

'Mmm, you are an early bird. You should have woken me.' She reached over and kissed him, and all his uncertainties melted away. She was as sure as he was that they had done the right thing and he couldn't find the words to describe how wonderful it made him feel to know that.

In the end he didn't bother trying. There were better ways to show her how he felt. He kissed her hungrily, groaning when his body made its own very blatant statement about how it felt. 'I'm sorry,' he said, attempting to put some space between them.

'Don't be.' She put her arms around him and smiled into his eyes. 'I can't think of a better way to start the day, can you?'

They made love with a passion that made a mockery of his fears. Katie didn't regret what they'd done last night or what they were doing this morning. She lay back against the pillow and sighed luxuriously once it was over.

'I could get used to this.'

'Me, too.' He dropped a kiss on her mouth. 'In fact, I have a suggestion. Neither of us has to go into work today so why don't we spend the day right here?'

'Here? You mean in bed?'

She sounded so shocked by the suggestion that he chuckled. 'Yes. I know it's a very decadent thing to do but I can't think of any place I'd rather be, can you?'

'No, I can't.' She sat up and kissed his bare shoulder. 'A day in bed with you sounds like heaven, Christos.'

'Good. I'll make us some breakfast, then.' He kissed her quickly on the lips then stood up. 'We'll need to keep our strength up.'

'With a bit of luck,' she agreed wickedly.

Christos laughed as he put on a robe. 'It's good to know that we agree on so many subjects.'

'Oh, we do, we do.' She tossed back the quilt. 'I think I'll have a shower while you make breakfast, if you don't mind.'

'Of course I don't mind.' He drew her into his arms and held her against him. 'In fact, I might join you once I've made our breakfast.'

'Something to look forward to,' she murmured, nuzzling his throat.

Christos sighed as she disappeared into the bathroom. He was very tempted to forget about breakfast and follow her.

Still, if he stuck to something simple, it shouldn't take too long to get everything ready.

He hurried downstairs and filled the coffee-maker then went out into the garden and picked some oranges for juice. Once the coffee and the juice were ready, all he had to do next was slice up some fruit and arrange it on a platter. The shower had stopped by the time everything was ready but maybe he could persuade Katie to have another shower after they'd eaten. They had a whole day to themselves so they could do exactly what they wanted.

The thought made him smile as he carried the tray along the hall. He was just about to take it upstairs when he heard a car draw up outside the villa. He frowned as he placed the tray on a table and went to the front door. He had no idea who could be calling at this hour of the morning but he would get rid of them as quickly as he could.

He opened the door and felt his stomach sink when he saw his cousin getting out of his car. What the hell was Petros doing here?

Katie had just stepped out of the shower when she heard a car draw up outside. She hurriedly towelled herself dry, feeling a little awkward at the thought of meeting Christos's visitor. It would be obvious that she had spent the night with him and she didn't want to cause him any embarrassment.

There was a robe hanging behind the bathroom door so she slipped it on and went to the window in time to see Petros climb out of his car. The shock of seeing him made her gasp. What on earth did he want at this time of the morning?

She left the bedroom and went to the top of the stairs, taking care that she couldn't be seen from below. She could tell from the tone of Christos's voice as he let his cousin in that he was no more pleased to see him than she was.

'What are you doing here?'

'What do you think?' Petros slammed the door. 'Why did you tell Eleni that I'd been seeing someone else? She's called off the wedding and told me that she never wants to see me again.'

'I have no idea what you're talking about,' Christos replied harshly. 'I haven't spoken to Eleni for several weeks.'

'Oh, come on! You don't expect me to believe that, do you?' Petros laughed. 'The only person who knew about me and Katie Carlyon was you, my dear cousin. I should have realised it was too much to hope that you'd keep your mouth shut. After all, you've been in love with Eleni for years so this must have seemed like the ideal opportunity to win her round. Did you tell her that I'd been seeing another woman in the hope that she would turn to you for comfort?'

Katie bit her lip as a searing pain lanced through her. Christos was in love with Eleni? Could it be true? She didn't want to believe it yet it explained so much about his attitude. She'd thought he had been trying to protect his cousin but it had been Eleni he'd been worried about. He'd been desperate to protect the woman he loved—maybe desperate enough to sleep with *her*? A wave of sickness rose up inside her. She couldn't bear to think that he had used her that way but she couldn't dismiss the idea.

'I did not tell Eleni about your affair,' Christos repeated in a voice like thunder. 'If she has found out, it had nothing to do with me.'

'Then Katie must have told her.' Petros swore harshly. 'I wish to heaven that I'd never got involved with her. I should have realised that she would cause trouble.'

Katie couldn't take any more. It was bad enough to discover that Christos had deceived he, without allowing his cousin to blacken her name again. 'How typical of you to blame everyone except yourself,' she said as she came down the stairs.

Petros swung round when he recognised her voice and his expression would have been comical if she hadn't been so angry. She stopped at the bottom of the stairs, steadfastly avoiding looking in Christos's direction. She didn't want to look at him and see the proof that it wasn't her he loved, didn't want to face the fact that he had used her as well. She had to deal with what was happening and worry about the rest later.

'Obviously, you're surprised to see me, Petros. Why? You must have known that your cousin would go the extra mile to ensure my co-operation or you wouldn't have enlisted his help.'

'Katie, that isn't true,' Christos said urgently, stepping forward. 'I know how it must appear, but you've got it all wrong.'

'I'm not interested in anything you have to say.' She barely glanced at him, knowing that she couldn't afford to weaken. She pinned Petros with an icy stare. 'I did not tell your fiancée about us. Is that clear?'

'But you must have done,' Petros blustered. 'Nobody else knew except the three of us.'

'Well, it wasn't me. If I'd wanted to tell her, I would have done so when I saw you at the hospital the other day.'

'You *saw* me?' Petros exclaimed.

'Yes. You were walking in the grounds and stopped right by the bench where I'd been eating my lunch.'

'I had no idea anyone had seen me…' He broke off and swallowed. 'Maybe it wasn't you after all,' he muttered.

'Right, that's just about enough.' Christos strode past him and flung open the door. 'I want you to leave. Now.'

Petros didn't wait to be told twice as he hurried out to his car. Katie clutched hold of the banister rail as her legs suddenly threatened to give way. The shock of what had happened was making her feel faint but she refused to make an even bigger fool of herself.

'Katie, I know what you must be thinking, but it isn't true.'

'Which bit?' She laughed. 'The fact that you have been in love with Eleni for years? Or that you slept with me to stop me causing trouble?'

'It wasn't like that!' Putting his hand under her elbow, he tried to lead her towards the sitting room. 'Let's sit down and talk about this—'

'No.' She shrugged off his hand, trying not to remember how she had felt last night and again that morning. His touch had thrilled her then but not any more. Now it made her feel sick to know that he had used her, just like his cousin had done. 'It seems perfectly clear to me, Christos. I even understand why you did it. Sleeping with me was a means to an end. I only hope that Eleni realises how much she means to you.'

'I did *not* sleep you with you to protect Eleni! You'd already told me that you were going back to England so why would I do such a thing? What would be the point?'

'Maybe you were afraid that I would tell her before I left—a sort of last-ditch attempt to pay Petros back for the way he'd treated me. But if you managed to *deflect* my interest onto you then I would be less likely to say anything to her.'

'That is complete and utter rubbish, and you know it is.' He captured her hands and held them tightly when she tried to pull away. 'Do you honestly think I could treat you like that after what we shared last night?'

'I don't know what to think, and is it any wonder? You never once told me that you were in love with Eleni, did you?'

'I didn't think it was necessary to tell you,' he said haughtily.

Katie's heart seemed to shrivel up. The fact that he'd not even tried to deny her accusation proved it was true. He *was* in love with Eleni and that confirmed her very worst fear, that last night had meant nothing to him.

She wrenched her hands free and Christos didn't try to stop her as she made her way upstairs. It only took her a few minutes to get dressed and when she went back down to the hall, he was waiting for her.

'I'll drive you into town. Just give me a couple of minutes to put on some clothes.'

'There's no need. I'll catch the bus if you'll tell me where it stops.'

He said something harsh under his breath. 'I've said that I will drive you home and that's what I shall do. I realise you are upset, Katie, and that this isn't the best time to sort things out, but the situation isn't as clear as you seem to believe.' He sighed when she didn't say anything. 'Stay here. I'll only be a couple of minutes.'

Katie sat down on the stairs because there was no point trying to leave when he would only come after her. She didn't want to cause a scene, certainly didn't want to do anything that might tip her over the edge. At the very least, she wanted to hold onto what was left of her dignity.

A feeling of numbness seemed to have enveloped her by the time he came back. She followed him out to the car and even thanked him when he opened the door for her. The drive back to town was completed in silence so it was a relief when he drew up outside the restaurant. It meant that she had to

endure only another few seconds of his company and then she
would be free to leave, or as free as she could be, bearing in
mind that she loved him. Tears welled to her eyes as she hurriedly reached for the doorhandle, but he was too quick for her.

'Please, don't leave like this, Katie. We need to talk about
what's happened. *I* need to explain—'

'No.' She turned brimming eyes to his face. 'Last night
was a mistake and I realise that now. I just want to forget it
ever happened.'

He drew back as though she had slapped him. 'In that case,
I won't detain you any longer.'

'Thank you.'

She got out of the car, not looking back as she hurried
across the pavement. She heard the engine roar as he drove
away and couldn't hold back her tears any longer. Hurrying
up to her room, she sat on the bed and cried as she had never
cried before—tears of pain and disillusionment. Christos was
in love with another woman and he didn't care about her. She
didn't know how she was going to carry on, knowing that he
would never love her as she loved him.

The week passed in a blur. Christos felt as though he was
locked into some sort of terrible nightmare from which he
couldn't escape. That Katie could have believed he had slept
with her to fulfil some hidden agenda of his own filled him
with despair. Surely she should have known how much that
night had meant to him? However, the fact that she believed
he was capable of making love to her while he was in love with
another woman simply proved how little she knew about him.

He took a couple of days off and spent them dealing with
a flurry of phone calls. It turned out that Petros had been

having an affair with a nurse who worked in the orthopaedic department. A friend of Eleni's had seen them together and had told Eleni. Apparently, it had been the nurse whom Katie had seen with Petros in the gardens that day.

Petros's parents were distraught when they found out why the wedding had been called off, but Christos refused to intercede. If his cousin could persuade Eleni to forgive him then all well and good, but he wasn't going to plead Petros's case. When Eleni herself telephoned and tearfully asked his advice, he gently explained that it must be her decision. He had no intention of getting involved again.

He didn't try to contact Katie because she had made it clear that she wasn't interested in anything he had to say. He consoled himself with the thought that she might have reconsidered her position by the time he went back to work, but in the event he discovered that she had opted to forfeit a week's pay rather than work out her notice. The rest of the staff were obviously surprised by her decision to leave so suddenly, but he refused to be drawn on the subject. He didn't want to discuss the mess he had made of his life with anyone.

Saturday arrived—the day Katie was due to leave. Christos had decided to work that day in the hope that it might take his mind off what was happening but he found himself constantly watching the clock. Her flight was due to leave at midday and as the morning passed, he grew increasingly restless. Should he let her go or should he try to stop her? But if he stopped her, what could he say? That he loved her and couldn't bear the thought of living without her? It was how he felt but he doubted if she would believe him now.

At five minutes past eleven he couldn't stand it any longer. He told Yanni that he had to go out and headed for the door.

However, he got no further than the car park when his pager started beeping. The code was the one they used for a major incident so he couldn't ignore it, yet he knew that if he responded, he wouldn't have a hope of reaching Katie before she boarded her plane.

In the end duty won, but it was the hardest thing he had ever done as he went back inside. He was letting Katie go and there was no way of knowing if he would see her again.

CHAPTER SIXTEEN

KATIE could hardly wait for Saturday to arrive. She just wanted to leave the island and put what had happened behind her. Christos hadn't made any attempt to contact her and that just proved how little she had meant to him. As she lugged her case into the airport, she knew that she would never return to Cyprus. This really was the end.

The terminal was crowded with holidaymakers making their way home. Katie joined the queue to check in her luggage but she hadn't reached the desk when there was an announcement over the Tannoy to say that all flights had been suspended. Pandemonium broke out as people tried to find out what was happening. However, it wasn't until one of the holiday reps explained that there was a problem with the undercarriage of a plane which was due to land that Katie realised how serious the situation was.

She decided to wait outside and left the terminal. She headed for the car park and sat down on a wall. She could hear sirens in the distance and realised that the emergency services had been summoned. Would there be a crew there from the hospital? And would Christos be with it? The thought that she might see him again aroused so many conflicting emotions.

She longed to see him one more time even though she knew there was no point.

The ambulances started to arrive a few minutes later and were waved through a side entrance leading to the runway. More vehicles quickly followed it. It was obviously a major incident and she couldn't help wishing that there was something she could do to help.

Another ambulance pulled up outside the car park and her eyes widened when she saw Christos climb out and run towards the terminal. Her heart started to beat in heavy, jerky thuds as she stood up. There was no reason to imagine that he was looking for her but she would only know that for certain if she spoke to him.

She hurried across the car park, knowing that she could be making a fool of herself, but she didn't care. Compared to the alternative—never seeing him again—it was a risk she was prepared to take. If there was a chance that she had made a mistake then she needed to find out before it was too late.

Christos scanned the crowd milling around inside the terminal. It seemed that fate had brought him to the airport after all. He was very aware that there were only a few minutes to spare before he had to get back to his team. The chances of him finding Katie amongst this crowd were extremely remote but he had to try. He would never forgive himself if he didn't make one last effort to sort things out between them.

His heart lurched when he saw a woman hurry into the building. Even though he only caught a glimpse of her, he recognised her immediately. He could feel himself trembling as he made his way through the crowd towards her because he had no idea how she was going to react. She didn't notice him at first but then she turned and saw him, and he knew in that moment that everything was going to be all right. Katie couldn't have looked at him that way if she didn't care about him!

The thought sent a flood of joy rushing through him. He didn't even pause to consider what he was doing as he gathered her into his arms. 'I never meant to hurt you,' he said hoarsely. 'I should have told you about Eleni right from the beginning. There's no time to explain it all to you now but I swear on my life that it's you I love and nobody else. Can you ever forgive me?'

'Yes.' She smiled up at him, her beautiful face alight with happiness. 'Of course I forgive you. I love you, too, Christos. So much.'

'Thank you.' He kissed her, knowing that he was the luckiest man alive to have been granted a reprieve. It was sheer torture to have to let her go when what he wanted most of all was to keep on holding her until he was sure that she knew how much he loved her. However, there were people depending on him and he couldn't let them down.

'I have to get back to my team. I don't know how long this is going to take but promise me that you won't leave. I know it's a lot to ask, but we need to talk, Katie, and clear up all these misunderstandings.'

'I'm not going anywhere.' She kissed him on the mouth then smiled at him. 'I'll be right here, waiting for you.'

He kissed her once more then dragged himself away while he was still capable of doing so. Everything was ready when he rejoined the team so there was nothing to do except pray as the stricken aircraft began its descent.

In the event the landing went far better than anyone had hoped it would. Although the fire engines were deployed, they weren't needed. The passengers used the emergency chutes to disembark. There were just half a dozen people injured and none of them was serious. An hour later they were ready to leave, although Christos didn't go with them. He had something to do first, something that couldn't wait any longer.

Katie was sitting on the steps outside the terminal when he went back to find her. She stood up when he appeared and stepped straight into his arms. Christos held her against his heart, knowing how close he had come to losing her. His voice was raw with emotion as he tilted her chin and looked into her eyes.

'I love you, Katie. I love you so very much.'

Tears welled to her eyes as she smiled at him. 'I love you, too.'

Christos felt his heart overflow with happiness and relief. That this beautiful, gentle woman had found it in her heart to forgive him was almost too much to take in. He felt as though he was floating on air and told her so.

Katie laughed in delight, loving the fact that he was willing to open his heart to her. 'I feel as though I'm on cloud nine as well,' she confessed.

'And that's where we're going to stay if I have my way,' he said firmly. He dropped another kiss on her lips then picked up her suitcase. 'I'll have to go back to work. Will you go to the villa and wait for me there? I'll try to get away as soon as I can. Promise.'

'Of course.'

She slipped her hand into his as they walked to the taxi rank, scarcely able to believe what was happening. The feeling of euphoria lasted all afternoon long, and it hadn't diminished by the time he came home. He took her in his arms and kissed her with a depth of love that proved how much he cared about her. Katie knew that she didn't need him to explain about Eleni or anything else, yet she sensed that he needed to tell her. When he sat her down on the sofa, she snuggled against him, wanting to make it as easy as possible for him.

'I know how hurt you were when Petros told you that I was in love with Eleni. I would have done anything to spare you that, my darling.'

'It did upset me,' she admitted, because it would be wrong to lie to him. Their relationship was too special, too precious, to allow for anything other than the truth between them.

'No wonder.' He kissed her on the forehead and sighed. 'That night we spent together was the most magical time of my entire life. I'd never felt like that with anyone before.'

'Neither had I.' She smiled shyly at him. 'I've not had that much experience, but when we made love I knew that it was unlike anything I had felt before.'

'Even with my cousin?' he said quietly.

'Especially with your cousin,' she said firmly, because she didn't want there to be any doubts about that.

Christos's eyes darkened as he pulled her into his arms. 'I wish there was some way I could make up for what he did to you, darling.'

'You already have. The fact that I would never have met you if it hadn't been for your cousin is all the compensation I need.' She kissed him tenderly. 'I don't care about the way he treated me. It's not important any more. I realise now that I was never really in love with him. I think I was flattered by the attention he paid me. I was also grieving for my father and that had a huge bearing on what happened, but I'm over him. You're all that matters to me now.'

'That's how I feel, too.' He ran his hand down her arm,

smiling when he felt her tremble. His voice was very deep when he continued. 'What I feel for you surpasses everything I ever felt for Eleni. Eleni and I went out together for a while after I qualified, but our relationship didn't work out.'

'It must have been hard for you,' she said quietly.

'It was.' He sighed. 'I was always very driven after my parents died. It was my way of compensating for what had had happened, I expect. When Eleni and I started seeing each other, I was in my first job and working punishingly long hours. I thought it would be all right because Eleni and I had grown up together and she knew how important my career was to me, but I expected far too much of her. It was inevitable that we would split up. It made me wary of making such a commitment again until I met you. When I met you, I realised that I wanted more from my life than just work.'

'So you're not still in love with Eleni?' she said hesitantly, hardly daring to believe that the explanation was so simple.

'No.' He kissed her softly. 'I love Eleni as a friend and I always will, but I'm not *in love* with her. I'm not sure if I ever was, to be honest. I certainly never felt the way about her that I feel about you.'

'I feel so sorry for her. She must be devastated by what's happened.'

'Oh, I'm sure that she and Petros will work things out eventually.' He sighed. 'It turned out that he had been seeing a nurse from the hospital. One of Eleni's friends saw them together and told Eleni.'

'No!' Katie gasped. 'I wonder if that was who he was with the day I saw him. I assumed he was with Eleni but I must have been mistaken. It doesn't matter now, although I'm glad it wasn't my fault that the wedding was called off.'

'I'm not sure if Eleni knows about you, although if I were Petros I would make sure that I told her about everything that has gone on. The only way to build a lasting relationship is through being honest with one another.'

'It is.' She smiled up at him. 'And I can honestly say that I love you, Christos.'

'And I love you, too.'

He kissed her again then stood up and held out his hand. Katie didn't hesitate as she placed her hand in his. Wherever he wanted to lead her, she was happy to follow. She would go to the ends of the earth to be with him.

He took her into his bedroom and made love to her with a tenderness that put a seal on their happiness. As she lay in his arms afterwards, she knew that she was the luckiest woman in the whole world. She had found her soul mate, the person who would always love and care for her and never let her down. She was just about to tell him that when she heard her mobile phone ringing.

She groaned. 'That's the downside of modern technology—people phone you at the most inauspicious times!'

Christos chuckled as he stood up. 'You stay there and I'll fetch your bag. That way we can carry on from where we left off.' He dropped a kiss on her nose. 'And while I'm gone try to decide what your answer is going to be.'

'What answer?'

'The one to this question: will you marry me?'

Katie gasped, but before she could think of anything to say, he left the room. She sank back against the pillow as a feeling of excitement filled her. She knew what her answer was going to be without needing to think about it.

He came back with her bag and sat down beside her. Katie

was all fingers and thumbs as she took out her phone because she was dying to tell him her answer. She smiled when she realised that it was her sister Kelly calling. It seemed right that she should share this very special moment with the other person in her life who mattered most to her.

'Hi, Kelly, I'm really glad you called. I have something to tell you.' She looked at Christos and smiled, holding his gaze as she continued. 'I'm getting married to the most wonderful man in the whole world!'

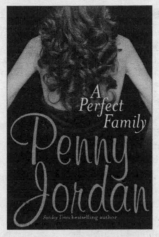

FREE

4 BOOKS AND A SURPRISE GIFT!

We would like to take this opportunity to thank you for reading this Mills & Boon® book by offering you the chance to take FOUR more specially selected titles from the Medical Romance™ series absolutely FREE! We're also making this offer to introduce you to the benefits of the Mills & Boon® Reader Service™—

- ★ **FREE home delivery**
- ★ **FREE gifts and competitions**
- ★ **FREE monthly Newsletter**
- ★ **Books available before they're in the shops**
- ★ **Exclusive Reader Service offers**

Accepting these FREE books and gift places you under no obligation to buy; you may cancel at any time, even after receiving your free shipment. Simply complete your details below and return the entire page to the address below. You don't even need a stamp!

YES! Please send me 4 free Medical Romance books and a surprise gift. I understand that unless you hear from me, I will receive 6 superb new titles every month for just £2.89 each, postage and packing free. I am under no obligation to purchase any books and may cancel my subscription at any time. The free books and gift will be mine to keep in any case.

M7ZEE

Ms/Mrs/Miss/Mr...Initials ....
BLOCK CAPITALS PLEASE

Surname ....

Address ....

....

....Postcode ....

Send this whole page to:

The Reader Service, FREEPOST CN81, Croydon, CR9 3WZ

Offer valid in UK only and is not available to current Mills & Boon® Reader Service™subscribers to this series.
Overseas and Eire please write for details. We reserve the right to refuse an application and applicants must be aged 18 years or over. Only one application per household. Terms and prices subject to change without notice. Offer expires 31st July 2007. As a result of this application, you may receive offers from Harlequin Mills & Boon and other carefully selected companies. If you would prefer not to share in this opportunity please write to The Data Manager at PO Box 676, Richmond, TW9 1WU.

Mills & Boon® is a registered trademark owned by Harlequin Mills & Boon Limited.
Medical Romance™ is being used as a trademark. The Mills & Boon® Reader Service™ is being used as a trademark.